PITFALLS AND PARACHUTES

PITFALLS AND PARACHUTES

A collection of short stories

By

DURGESH SHASTRI

PARTRIDGE
A Penguin Company

Copyright © 2013 by Durgesh Shastri.

ISBN:	Hardcover	978-1-4828-0142-2
	Softcover	978-1-4828-0143-9
	Ebook	978-1-4828-0141-5

Sketches by Ashok Ramdhani

Partridge books may be ordered through booksellers or by contacting:

Partridge India
Penguin Books India Pvt.Ltd
11, Community Centre, Panchsheel Park, New Delhi 110017
India
www.partridgepublishing.com
Phone: 000.800.10062.62

Contents

To,

My Mother
&
Chidambar

PREFACE

The foundation for writing the book was laid way back in 2006. I used to stay alone in Bangalore during those days. Reading fiction was my passion, and an activity to pass the time. Slowly, I began writing my own stuff using pen and paper. This gradually transformed into writing blogs. The enthusiastic response of my online friends drove me towards writing more. Fiction is something which has always interested me. Some of the interesting ideas and situations which I encountered during the course of these eight years are presented in the form of PITFALLS AND PARACHUTES.

My engineering background has been my strength. The experience I gained during my short stint in an IT company has been handy in writing some of the stories. During the course of writing this book, I've realized that any situation in life can be turned to one's advantage. Tougher and difficult situations always make for an interesting and exciting story. The Hyderabad bloggers meet that I attended in January 2012 served as a stimulant and played a vital role in taking the writing process forward.

This collection of short stories is carefully handpicked from a larger private collection of mine. I always believed in writing stories, which take the reader on an unforgettable journey. Entertainment is at the core of the stories. Humor and exciting endings are something which I can't do without. Read the stories and list your favorite ones. You can let me know your choices and feedback by sending emails. Any suggestions or criticism is always welcome. Hope the stories entertain you as much as they entertained me during the writing process.

Place: Bidar
Date: 11/06/2013

ACKNOWLEDGEMENTS

I would like to thank Mr. Sidney Sheldon whose biography on History channel awakened the writer in me. *A story is not made by a plot. It is made by interesting characters put together in unusual situations*, he said. Thus began my writing journey.

My mother has been a source of inspiration. She was the first to read my stories during the past five years since I began writing on the internet. She has been an admirer and a critic of my writings. This book wouldn't have been possible without her timely feedback.

I am grateful to my family, especially my father and brother Rajesh, for they always believed that I had the potential to write a book. I am also grateful to my friends for sparing me the necessary time to write the book. They have also been supportive in many ways than one.

I would like to mention few people whose constant admiration of my work kept the writer in me alive. They are Venkateswaran P.S, Kamalji, Kanak Rekha Chauhan, Deena Bhat, Kavi, Praveen, Harsh Puri, Panchali Sengupta, Aneet Bariya, Hetav Dave, Veena Desai, D.Sampath, G. Raghava Reddy, Dr. Shantala, Navneet Bakshi, Ravikanth, Shivshanker Sastry, Ghazala, Bina Gupta, and Prof. Afroze Pasha.

I would like to thank the computer science department of GNDEC for its encouragement and support.

I would also like to thank the Sulekha family. Sulekha Rivr made me feel like a celebrity. It provided me a platform to showcase my writing skills and get noticed by some of the best writers in India. I will always be indebted to Rivr.Sulekha.com.

My wife, Sunita has been instrumental in handling the household chores. She was supportive throughout the writing phase. Her enthusiastic response on reading my stories made me write even better.

I would like to thank the team at partridge publishing, which helped turn my dream into a reality.

Last but not the least I would like to thank Sadhguru Shri. Jaggi Vasudevji. The Inner Engineering program I attended provided me the necessary energy, focus, and sense of balance needed for the completion of this book. It has changed my life in many ways than one. Without Sadhguru's blessings and grace, I wouldn't have boarded the parachute of my writing career.

THE LOST LADY

I worked for an American company named Jacksoft Pvt Ltd. It had three branches in India at Pune, Chennai, and Bangalore. The Bangalore branch where I worked as the director was under loss for quite some time. The bosses at America had decided to assess the operations at the Bangalore center and take an appropriate decision after a visit. They were on a truth finding mission to analyze why this center was in loss when the others made sizeable profit. Mr. Graham and Mr. Luke had come all the way from Tennessee, U.S. and were residing at the Leela palace. They were scheduled to visit our office at 8:00 A.M. accompanied by Mr. Natarajan, CEO, operations India and a few other Indian delegates. I and Mr. Shreepad Nambodripad were responsible for operations at the Bangalore center. Shreepad was more experienced than me and was the divisional head.

Previous night we had chalked out our strategy and had reviewed our power point presentation to impress the foreign bosses. Lack of manpower was the main cause of us making losses, Shreepad pointed out. We were short of the required skilled resources, hence failed to meet targets and had to delegate work elsewhere, he concluded. Four people's job was being done by one person, resulting in delay, in meeting deadlines. The power point consisted of attractive graphs and tables. It also had a comparison chart which highlighted several differences among the various Indian centers. The fate of the 30 odd employees who worked at our center rested on how tactfully we would handle the situation and impress the bosses for hiring more skilled employees. Shreepad was all geared up for the presentation. We looked forward to the next day with hope. The office was at a distance of 10 km from my home, and approximately it took half an hour to reach.

"Honey, get ready soon!" my wife woke me up at around 6:30 A.M. I had one hour's time to get ready. My morning chores included bringing milk and newspaper from a nearby point, dropping my daughter to school and then heading straight to the office. I headed straight to the milk store in my t-shirt and shorts. I planned to be at least 15 minutes early at the office on that particular day. But who would have anticipated that this journey from home to the milk store was going to be the most difficult journey of my life. It had nearly cost me my job and reputation.

After crossing a few lanes, I encountered an old lady. She had a bent back and wore a stressed look. She might have been in her seventies. She came for a morning walk and lost her way. The weak lady begged for help. In spite of Bangalore being such a planned city, people many times lose their way. Finding her home would have been easy if she had remembered the address or her husband's or son's phone number. But the only thing she remembered was that she stayed in a white building. Many houses in the locality were white colored. She confirmed that she had lost her way barely after a 15 minutes' walk from her home. I felt sorry for the poor lady and decided to help her out. Probably, it was the first mistake of that morning.

We walked in the eastern direction for 10 minutes and even knocked on few of the doors, but it yielded no result. Walking wasn't a wise decision after all I thought, and decided to board an auto rickshaw to save time. This was the second mistake of that morning. Luckily we got one immediately. I directed him to look for a white building in the surrounding. That guy seemed extremely enthusiastic and entered every nook and corner, taking us to every white building that came our way. The poor old lady failed to recognize any of them. After a 30 minute journey, he stopped at one point. This search had landed us into a different area altogether. My watch clocked 7:15. I was now getting restless. I had to be in the office at 8:00 A.M at any cost.

"Sir I have taken you to every possible white building. Kindly pay me my bill of 80 rupees. I can't go any further," the driver said.

"What do you mean, you can't go further? You have misled us. Take us back to the place from where we started," I said.

"I am not going in that direction any longer. Pay my bills and get down!" he said loudly. Auto drivers can sometimes be highly stubborn. I got down the auto along with the old lady and soon realized that we were not meant to take different routes, not at least in the near future. I only had 20 rupees in my pocket. I wasn't carrying my cell phone either. The only thing in my possession was the wrist watch which my wife had gifted me on our anniversary.

"See I have only twenty rupees with me. Try to understand. Drop us at Jayanagar 9th block and I would pay you the entire money," I pleaded.

"You can't force me to go places!" he thundered. "Pay me or else be willing to visit the police station."

This guy was willing to drag me to a police station for mere 80 rupees. I warned him to control his tongue. I wasn't of the kind to dupe people.

"You don't know who I am. Do as I say and I shall pay you," I tried to convince him.

He gave it a thought and agreed to take us back. But we needed to first visit the petrol pump where he would replace the existing LPG cylinder in the auto with a new one. It would take 5 minutes, he suggested. He even demanded 500 rupees for forcing him to take us back. I was running short of time and agreed to his demand. My head rolled on spotting a beeline of autos at the petrol pump waiting to get their LPGs replaced.

"This will take half an hour, and I can't afford to waste time here," I screamed at him.

"Pay me my money and get lost!" he shouted. It was really a test of patience. It was 7:30 A.M already. I remained silent for some time and requested for his cell phone. My wife would be really worried. Her missing husband had not even performed his daily morning rituals. I had to inform her. But the auto driver straight away rejected my request citing 'zero balance' in his mobile phone as the reason. I couldn't waste any more time there as it would take at least 20 minutes if not less. I decided to sacrifice the only useful gadget I had. It was the most beautiful gift by my wife. She would inquire about it definitely, in case she found it missing. I would purchase a new one before she even noticed it. The watch cost not less than 3000 rupees. It was a Timex Fastrack. The coolest watch which adored my wrist.

I asked the lady to be seated in the auto and invited the driver in one corner. I explained him how precious the watch was and offered it to him, also explaining him how important it was for me to return home. His stubborn attitude could cost me my job. He would get anywhere around 2000 rupees by selling it. He carefully examined it for few minutes determined to prove that it was fake. I requested him to hurry. He had secret discussions with his friends who were in the queue. One of them approached and handed me his watch. It looked exactly like mine. He asked me to guess its cost. I failed miserably when he revealed that it cost him only 60 rupees.

"There are a number of watch sellers in Bangalore who sit by the road side and sell designer fake watches for unbelievable rates. Yours is no better that those," he remarked.

"Thank you my friend. He had almost cheated me by making me believe his words," said my auto driver (to his friend) and then stared at me with a wicked grin as if trying to convey that he was smart enough not to be fooled by a donkey like me.

"But mine is the original, believe me!" I tried to convince them.

"We see many fakers like you every day," one of them said.

It was 7:45 A.M already. I tried to regain my cool. Even as I was negotiating with them, the old lady approached us.

"I have been watching you two since then. I have understood that you are not interested in searching my home. I will take you to police!" she warned me. I remained speechless trying to regain my composure.

"Your gang wants to sell me and trade my organs," she continued.

I tried diverting my attention from the nonsense which I just heard. I found myself in the mess just because I tried to help her. She was now accusing me of selling her vital organs. If only all her organs functioned properly, she wouldn't have lost her way. 'Nobody would be interested in buying those useless organs' I wanted to hit back but remained quiet.

"No, Amma, I am not a part of his gang. I really want to help you," the auto driver pleaded innocence.

"I am a director of a reputed company. I don't belong to any gang!" I said.

Just when all doors seemed closed, and I felt I was in deep waters, something flashed. It was the same petrol pump where I filled fuel in my car on several occasions. I was now at a distance of less than 2 km from my office. In search of the old lady's home, we had traveled a distance of almost 8 km. I begged him to take me to the Jacksoft Pvt Ltd office at Koramangala. I assured the old lady that she would be safe, and it was just a matter of time before she was back with her family. She reluctantly agreed but warned me against any misadventures and told me that she would scream loudly if I involved myself in any suspicious activity again. Other auto drivers clicked my photo hurriedly using their cell phones and assured her that they would hand it over to police, in case she failed to reach her home soon. I failed to understand how they would know if she reached or not but I pretended as if their ploy had scared me. The driver fitted a new cylinder and was back quickly. We had waited for almost 30 minutes. I reached the office sharp at 7:55 A.M.

The sight of their director reaching the office in shorts and T-shirt shocked the employees', who had all gathered outside to welcome the foreign bosses. I looked as if I were straight out of my bed to office. My undone hairs added to the skimpy look. The fact that I came in an auto and the sight of an old lady made them even more curious. They surely believed that I needed my mother's blessings that day.

The delegates arrived exactly at 8:00 A.M along with the CEO and a few other Indian authorities. I welcomed them with a broad smile. The smile on their faces faded at the first glimpse of me. "He wanted to welcome you all very differently. That's why this sporty look," said the CEO, Mr. Natarajan. He laughed and said, "Well done, gentleman," while shaking hands with me. The look on his face clearly stated that he was clueless. He stared at me as if asking are you mad.

The receptionist gestured that there were several calls from my home inquiring about my whereabouts. I just nodded. Mr. Natarajan took them to the boardroom for the presentation. I borrowed some money from a colleague and paid the auto driver. He left as soon as he received the payment. I instructed the old lady to wait in the lounge and not to create any scene until my return. She ordered me to return in the next 30 minutes. There was a huge clock hanging on the wall. She sat there staring at it. I entered the boardroom to the right side of the lounge. The trauma for the day had not yet ended. There was no presentation to be showcased. Shreepad had prepared it and had not yet arrived at the office, citing some emergency. Mr. Natarajan, Luke, and Graham were shaking their heads in disagreement. The anger on the CEO's face was clearly evident.

"Such carelessness cannot be tolerated. I now realize why the state of affairs is so pathetic at this center!" said Luke. "What's use of providing more manpower when the existing one is such?" he questioned.

Every eye looked in my direction expecting some explanation. I had to speak up. I narrated the tragic events that led me coming to the office in such attire. There was silence after that. Mr. CEO sympathized with me. The Indian bosses assured the two foreign bosses that they knew how dedicated, staff at the Bangalore center was. It was already 8:30 and there was still no sight of Shreepad. Just when I decided to call (from the office phone) him, the door opened, and the old lady stood there in fury.

"So you plan to sell me off to these foreigners?" She thundered.

"Listen to me," I said. Luke and Graham exchanged unpleasant looks. They were being branded as a part of an international mafia gang which specialized in organ trading, by her.

"I should have known what your evil intentions were. Chotu had warned me against talking to or seeking help from any stranger in the city. It was my mistake that I approached you," she went on. She scared for her life.

"No, Amma listen to us," Mr. CEO tried to calm her down. Natarajan tried consoling and approached her but ended up receiving a tight slap in return. The sound resonated in every corner of the room followed by pin drop silence. I was terrified. I looked for a suitable place, to hide myself. The very next moment the door opened again, and this time it was my wife along with my sweet daughter.

"Thank God you are alright!" she said.

"Oh honey, I was about to call you."

"We have been through hell since morning. You had gone to fetch milk, and I find you in office! How can you be so careless, my little pony?" she said and came running in my arms unable to control her emotions. All my top bosses now knew my secret pet name. It looked as if the people there had gathered to witness two estranged lovers meet after a ground breaking struggle.

The old lady stood in silence and utter disbelief. The person whom she considered being a leader of an international organ trading gang was embracing his lovely wife and daughter. He was a traditional Indian family man. The scene moved her, and she was in tears. She dropped at the feet of Natarajan and begged for his forgiveness possibly realizing her mistake. In all humbleness, he made her stand. He explained that she was like his mother. He even turned his other cheek towards her indicating that she was free to slap him again if she wished to. He had no other choice but to be magnanimous before others. She hit him gently, and everyone smiled. Natarajan took it upon himself and assured her that she soon would be home.

The very next moment Shreepad entered the room looking sad and stressed.

"My apologies gentlemen, but it was an emergency. In fact, it is . . ." he said in a low voice and was cut short before he could complete.

"Chotu!" screamed the old lady. Since she was facing the other members in the room, Chotu hadn't seen her face. She recognized him through his voice.

"Mom, Thank god you are safe. I mean what a surprise!" the sadness had turned into ecstasy. Tears of joy began flowing from his eyes. I now recalled the white building the old lady was referring to. I had been there many times. She had arrived in the city only yesterday and Chotu alias Shreepad had mentioned it. He had even sighted that the presentation would be a grand success as he had his mother's blessings. I finally heaved a sigh of relief. The emotionally charged atmosphere had energized everyone. Mr. Luke stood up and clapped, others followed him.

"Love, respect and humility are the values which make Indians great," he remarked. Everyone else nodded in agreement. No doubt we impressed them with our presentation, reasoning, and also successfully saved our jobs.

THE END

REALITY BITES

Reality shows have conquered the Indian television market very recently. People have developed the taste for reality shows. Popular actors from the film industry host these shows and publicize them. The winner of reality TV gets away with lakhs or crores of rupees. Everybody involved in the production of the show makes money. The host walks away with lakhs together for a single episode. The customers end up losing some money in the process of voting for their favorite contestants. The reality market is such that even a sleeping person's video can be a big blockbuster if presented properly. From philosophy to wrestling, cricket to stock market, round the clock news to cookery shows, everything is marketed in real time on TV in today's world. Smart presentation is the need of the hour. Some news channels go to the extent of fabricating something interesting and presenting it as reality. Such channels end the show inconclusively. Most people don't know where their life is headed. That's the reality of life including mine.

I stayed alone in a single bedroom house at Banashankari 3rd stage, Bangalore. I was a civil engineer having completed my graduation from the same city. Lush green gardens surrounded the area. I had completed construction projects while successfully working as a junior engineer for a firm named Aditya builders. *Building your dream home* was our tagline. We acquired lands at market rates from prospective sellers and erected huge commercial establishments. My family was based in a small village in the northern part of Karnataka. At 30, I was the most eligible bachelor of my village. Parents of many prospective brides had approached my family for an alliance. But I had shown the slightest interest. My father doubted if I had a running affair. He could find no other reason for me to reject the proposals. I had made it clear that I would select the girl of my choice if they like it or not.

When all my friends were after beautiful and curvy girls, my obsession was girls with an intoxicating voice. I longed for someone who could sing melodiously and spread sugary sweetness around with her voice. I was ready to compromise on looks, and never cared about a girl's parental property or her bank balance. The popular Bollywood singers, who fit the criteria, were out of my reach. During my stay in Bangalore, I fell in love with a popular city RJ. She was Joanna. I even visited her once in office. I had detailed information concerning the show that she hosted. I had gathered all her personal information related to family and friends. Information related to her favorite hangout spot, hobbies, and favorite pass time activity was at my finger tips.

I had met Joanna a little late. She was engaged to a far richer guy and considered me her biggest fan. She loved him immensely. I didn't want to play spoilsport either. The short love story ended with heartbreak. My second crush was the owner of my previous house. Every morning she sang bhajans and I woke up on hearing her melodious voice. We used to see each other daily as she stayed just adjacent to my room. But the problem was that she was already married. I enquired if she had a sister with a similar voice, and came to know that she had a younger brother who was aspiring to be an Indian idol. I had not come across any other lady with a voice similar to hers. My family, friends, & neighbors considered it a bizarre criterion for marriage. My search was on for the past five years.

It was around 10 A.M. on a lazy Sunday morning that I decided to visit the Srivastava family. The Srivastavas were obsessed with reality TV. They were my neighbors since 2 years. Their appetite for reality shows had only grown stronger. The family consisted of an octogenarian couple, their son Prashanth, daughter-in-law Sheela, and their kids of 8 and 6 years, Amar and Rachna. Everyone had a different taste for reality shows. The lazy Sunday can be turned into a really exciting day if exciting people are around. I visited them quite often. During which they behaved normally. But on this particular Sunday, things were different. I was warmly welcomed by the grandpa who opened the door.

A plate of potato chips, moong dal, and Thums up was placed on the table right next to the cushioned sofa where the grandpa was seated.

'India's got huge talent' the talent hunt show's auditions had begun. An 80 year old man was singing the famous 'Kolaveri Kolaveri di' in a shaky voice, dancing, and exhibiting his talent. He was accompanied by an old lady. The guy further produced some instrumental sounds, mimicked the whistle of a train, and the take off of an airplane. This was followed by a thunderous applause by the audience. They were full of laughter. This was not the kind of talent to be showcased on the National television. The audience respected his age. His wife appreciated him saying that his entire life was dedicated for singing.

The judges rejected the aged man. They sarcastically said that he was far bigger than the stage. The old man was proud of his achievement, he missed the context. This brought sweet memories back in the grandpa seated next to me. Tears appeared in those eyes. Chidanand Srivastava, the grand old man of the family, loved giving unwarranted comments. He was totally unpredictable. Whether the other person liked it or not, he would say what he wanted.

"What happened grandpa?" I asked. He took a sip of the cold drink and replied.

"The guy who just performed was my junior during graduation days. When I see young lads like him perform, I tend to get emotional. He was an average singer then. His only desire in life was to be on TV one day. Today he has achieved it," he said and burped loudly.

That wasn't an achievement by any means. He had only fulfilled his deepest desire. But he had done no justice to his singing talent, in case he had any.

"Even newly born kids appear on TV these days, what's the big deal?" I said. My straight talk had not gone down well with the grandpa.

"He is much younger than you at heart," grandpa declared while taking another sip. Why compare me with a failed singer? I don't even sing in the bathroom. Neither did I ever dream of becoming a Mohd. Rafi.

"There can be no comparison between us," I said a little angrily. He had not offered me any of the snacks that he was consuming so joyously.

"See how easily you surrendered. Dream big and work towards it. You will be successful one day like my junior," he gave a free unsolicited advice. He had totally missed the point. But I was not in a mood to argue.

"Thanks for the suggestion," I said.

"You know I was a teacher in the primary school. I was adjudged the best teacher in school by my colleagues. But nobody recognizes my contribution. Lots of my students are in high positions, and they appear on TV often; I gave them the strictest of punishments so that they chased their dreams. Today TV is making it happen. When you are on TV, the whole world recognizes you. I've prepared individuals on whom the nation can rely upon," he said. This was the first time in the day I felt pity on him. It hurts when you go unrecognized.

"You have so wonderful and loving family. You should be proud of them," I said changing the topic.

"The sad part is they don't listen to me. My ideas, advises, and achievements are all outdated!" he said painfully.

"We the younger generation has a lot to learn from you," I said consoling him.

"Then chase your dreams. I want to see you on TV one day," he said.

"It isn't a yardstick for somebody's achievement," I said.

"What's your dream?" he asked.

"I don't dream," I said. Our discussion had reached a deadlock. His question had triggered a chain of thoughts in me. My favorite subject in school was biology especially botany. I loved plants and nature. My dream was to be a gardener. Our college gardener Mahadevappa was my icon. He spent much of his time in trimming the plants and giving them nice shapes. I liked the blossoming of the flowers. It's a treat to watch. When it was time to choose a career, I preferred engineering. My profession was clearing the grounds and constructing sky rocketing buildings. I am one of the several skilled people, who are working day and night to turn this lovely planet into a concrete jungle. I hated it. But it was necessary for my survival. I often got nightmares where in the planet was left with no forests. I was scared to sleep. Dreaming was a big no.

"You are in need of some eye opening discourses, to make you dream," he said. The contradicting statement confused me for a moment.

"How can one dream by opening one's eyes?" I wanted to ask but remained quiet.

"Ever heard of Baba Jagruthi? The great spiritual master!" he said. How can someone, with a beautiful name of a girl, be a spiritual master? I had never heard of him.

"Funny name he he," I laughed. Grandpa gave a stern expression.

"He is the most celebrated and recognized master of present times. Everyone recognizes him because of JAAGO TV," he said. The TV was now tuned to JAAGO Channel. The baba in white robes had a long white beard with selected strands of dark brown and that looked stylish. The Baba definitely had a taste. He wore a traditional head gear with JAAGO written on it. He was dancing with some of his devotees on a popular devotional song. Grandpa looked at the screen intently.

"He failed in every exam; he was the most mischievous of the lot. He chased his dreams. See the result. You can observe the same mischievousness in his dance," he said. The Baba was forcing one of the reluctant female devotees to join him by holding her hand. His only focus seemed to be her. "You must listen to one of his discourses too."

"Pyaar kiya toh darna kya, jab pyaar kiya toh darna kya, pyaar kiya koi chori nahi ki," suddenly this song was audible from the adjacent room. I looked at grandpa in surprise.

"That is Sharada," he said proudly. Sharada was his wife.

"Even she is chasing her dreams. She's preparing for the auditions of the reality singing contest 'Rock star granny of India'. She suffers from asthma yet she's hopeful of being selected. Her adamant father had stopped her from singing. She had sacrificed her interest for the sake of family. I revived her interest in singing recently."

"I wish her all the best," I said.

"When will you give us a chance to wish you in something worthwhile?" he shot back. I absorbed it. Why was he so concerned about me?

I saw sweet Rachna running towards the grandpa, "What happened to my doll?" he asked.

"Mommy beat me. She is bad!" the girl was screaming.

"Mommy isn't evil. She loves you. Tell me what happened," grandpa said.

"I was singing Sheela ki jawani," she said and cried more loudly.

I geared up to take Rachna's side. Why would the mother be offended if a blockbuster song is penned after her name? What was the girl's mistake?

"Sing some other song dear, there are several beautiful ones," he said.

"No, I like this only. Sheela ki jawani . . ." she began loudly as if inviting her mother to beat her again, the old man would rescue her this time.

Sheela didn't come, but Amar came running and hit her on the head. He was a Momma's boy.

"You don't interfere. Go wrestle with your friends!" she told him angrily.

"You stop singing that nasty song or else I will choke slam you," Amar said raising his hand high above his head. Choke slam is a popular stunt in wrestling, using which the wrestler lifts the opponent by his neck high in the air and dumps him on the ground, within seconds.

"He thinks he is the great Khali. Idiot doesn't know that choke slam is a signature move of the undertaker," Rachna said. I appreciated her knowledge of the WWE.

Sheela entered the hall. She was preparing the lunch. "Good morning Cyrus!" she greeted me. I greeted her with a smile. Seeing her was a welcome relief compared to chatting with the old man.

"The TV has made the entire family mad," said an irritated Sheela. The naughty Rachna ran away in the bedroom humming Sheela ki jawani.

"The idiot box is a dream realizing instrument these days," I said taking a pot shot at the grandpa. He dropped a large potato chip which he was about to eat, back in the plate.

"What is meant by an idiot box grandpa?" Amar asked curiously.

"Some idiots who don't know the importance of TV call it that way," he said staring at me.

"TV is father-in-law's best means of time pass nowadays. He doesn't tolerate someone abusing his best buddy, the TV. When we asked him to become spiritual, he developed a keen interest in JAAGO TV," said Sheela clarifying his recent remark on me.

"One can never become spiritual by watching TV," I hit back.

"Even I agree with Cyrus," she said.

"I pity you ignorant beings," said grandpa.

"Consuming a cold drink is ignorance. Eating chips also is ignorance," I said. He burped louder than ever. The cold drink bottle was now empty. Realizing her folly Sheela headed for the kitchen, to fetch me some snacks. "This kitchen work keeps me so busy that I even forget to treat the guests," she mumbled.

"What is my Undertaker doing?" grandpa asked Amar sweetly. Amar was trying to hold my neck in his tiny palm.

"Grandpa how many times to tell you I am not Undertaker. I am the great Khali!" he said, "I am trying to choke slam uncle."

"That's why I said TV is an idiot box. Keep away from me," I warned him.

"Uncle is scared, uncle is scared!" he said loudly. Sheela was back with my snacks.

"Today Mommy is preparing a Rajasthani dish inspired by the Master Chef kitchen!" he said.

"Yeah Cyrus, you can join us today for lunch. Amar has warned that if the dish lacks in taste then its fate will be the dustbin, and they will all remain hungry as a mark of protest. Today is a test of my cooking abilities."

Food enters the dustbin if it doesn't meet the standards in some of the cookery shows.

"Thank you for the invitation," I said.

There was a knock on the door. It was Prashanth. He was in his early forties. He carried a parcel containing fruits and milk.

"Good morning Cyrus!"

"Good morning!" I replied.

"Kindly switch to some news channel," he told his dad.

"You watch the news every day, but you are never in the news. I had grand hopes from you," said grandpa. 'Was it necessary for the old man to give his expert opinion about everything?' I asked myself.

"Father, do what I say!"

The TV was tuned to Moon news channel. Breaking news caught the attention of everyone in the large hall. A poor eight year old boy attempted to steal a burger being parceled into IT Company in Whitefield. The security guards beat up the boy very badly. His mother was abused when she tried to rescue him. The company had filed a case of trespassing and robbery against the poor chap. The boy was admitted to a government hospital in a critical condition.

"If only she had given the right direction to him, things would have been different," said grandpa.

"She seems to have no money even to decently cover her. Look at her torn clothes. Survival is the biggest thing for them," I said.

Prashant and Sheela nodded in agreement.

"Amar wanted to throw the food in dustbin. Do you realize how irresponsible that was?" Sheela asked him. He remained silent.

The TV reporter next spoke to the helpless mother.

"What triggered your son to steal things?"

"We are not thieves' sahib!"

"Can you tell us what exactly transpired?"

The emotional lady began narrating her background, "My husband was an alcoholic. He died two years ago. He worked as an auto rickshaw driver. The auto was on loan . . . ."

"Tell us about the incident," said the insensitive and impatient reporter.

She ignored him, ". . . . . After his death, the bank seized the auto. We couldn't afford the rent and were forced to spend our nights on railway station and footpaths. My son's schooling stopped."

"Everybody has a bitter experience of life at some point in time. Tell us about the incident, tell us how you turned to robbery!" he interrupted.

"I want the world to know about the everyday struggle of people like us. Are we not humans?"

The reporter was silent.

"We don't have anybody to look after our selves. I visit shops every day and sing songs. Then I ask them to give me something for my performance. Sahib, I want to clarify that we are neither beggars nor thieves. Past two days have been worse. We ate the leftovers from the dustbins around the city. The security guard had promised me that if I sang well then he would give me the parcel that he was carrying for his boss. He made me sing different songs of his liking. I did as he said. In the end, he refused to give me my due. He abused me. My angry son couldn't bear the injustice. He forcefully tried to snatch it from the guard, and in a fit of rage the guard beat him." She was in tears.

"So this is the plight of the poor in namma (our) city Bangalore," said the news reader.

A number of women and child rights groups had come forward to help the victims. They demanded the immediate arrest of the guard. The grandma in the Srivastava family was singing to fulfill her desire. And here was a lady for whom singing on streets was her life's necessity.

"Society needs to change," said Prashanth.

"Then do something about it!" said grandpa.

"What can I do?" he said.

"Why don't you sponsor the child's education?"

"I find it difficult to make ends meet for my family. Charity can wait."

"What about you?" grandpa asked me.

"What can I do? A number of human rights groups have already come forward for help," I said.

"I know you can be useful in a big way."

Was he hinting that I should marry that lady and adopt her child? After all, she was a singer.

Suddenly the TV played a sports channel.

"Hey wrestling is on," said an elated Amar.

"Give me the remote," said Prashant and a verbal duel ensued between the two.

I excused myself to leave. Sheela reminded me about the lunch invitation at 1:30 P.M. "You have not even eaten the snacks properly," she remarked as I geared up to leave.

"Sure I will be on time," I said half heartedly and left.

However hard I tried it was difficult not to think of that poor lady. Grandpa's words swirled in my mind. What was he hinting at? The lady was young. She looked attractive. She was widowed. Her only son was in hospital battling for life. She was in need of help, not financially but emotionally. But above all she was a gifted singer. Her voice had a certain magnetic pull in it. It attracted me towards her. She also had self respect.

Amar knocked on the door, reminding me about the lunch invitation. They were waiting for me. I faked a headache and apologized for my last minute non-availability. Sheela parceled me food the next moment along with some tablets for my headache. From the news reports, it was clear that the female resided close to Whitefield, some 35 km from my place. The boy was admitted in the government hospital nearby which was easy to locate. The afternoon was exhausted in understanding her background and current status based on media reports. The evening was used up in understanding the pros and cons of my decision. My parents would be angry, but someday they would unquestionably be proud of my decision. What would the society think of me?

During the night, I made a decision. Early in the morning I visited the hospital. A sobbing helpless mother was weeping over her fate and praying for the son's safety. From a distance, she looked different than in the TV. No human rights group, which had pledged support for her on TV, was visible at the hospital.

I assured that her problems would vanish soon. She only needed to believe.

"Everyone shows fake sympathies and gives false assurances. He is my only hope," she said.

"Even I hope that he will be soon alright. We can only pray for his speedy recovery," I said, "But there is something else which I can do for you." She gave a puzzled expression.

Six months later.

"Raju your Tiffin is ready!" said Anuja his mother. An excited Raju was all geared up to go to school. It was his first day after all.

Anuja couldn't believe that she had a permanent house of her own. The two rooms meant a lot to her. She conveyed her heartfelt gratitude for whatever I had done. That was the least I could do being a civil engineer & someone involved in real estate. It required some investment, but in turn it gave immense satisfaction. As far as my melody queen was concerned. The hunt continued.

THE END

TAINTED REPUTATION

The past was knocking on his door as he brewed his coffee. He knew it was her nephew. The guy wouldn't let him even prepare a cup of coffee, let alone sip it. There was another knock within seconds.

"Bastards!" he murmured and stood up. The servants had not turned up for work that day. They didn't value him as they did some time ago. The hot coffee cup found its way on the dining table. He sluggishly headed towards the door. There was another knock in the mean time.

"Have patience you fool!" he said while opening the door. Comfort, peace and happiness had quietly exited his life all because of his wrong choices.

"Hello Mr. Pramanik," said the curly haired cute young boy of ten. The boy had the charm to mesmerize anyone. He glanced at the boy rather angry and irritated. It was Arjun, nephew of Mr. Pramanik's neighbor Ranjana. "Aunt needs a glass of milk as she's expecting some guests," he said adorably.

"You think I run a dairy farm or something?"

"Don't be so rude uncle," the boy smiled and said endearingly.

Just get lost, he wanted to say but headed towards the kitchen.

The refrigerator contained only one packet of milk. He found the boy occupy one of the chairs of the dining table on return. This drove him furious. "Who invited you inside? Learn some manners you fool!" he screamed. The boy remained silent.

"Take this packet!" Pramanik handed over the milk packet and squeezed the boy's cheeks while maintaining a steely smile. Those soft cheeks turned red. The child gave an innocent sympathetic look. He pinched the little boy's lips and held the child's jaw, pressing it with his giant palm. The neck was tender and attractive, but Pramanik controlled his aggression. The scared boy headed towards the exit without a word. Pramanik followed him to close the door.

Pramanik was a student leader in college. His leadership skills landed him into the world of politics. He entered politics with the intention of cleansing the society of its evil practices. He soon became a major political party's youth leader and acquainted a beautiful woman, Mangala. His opponents only waited for an opportunity to tarnish his image. The marriage was fixed, and his wealthy father-in-law gave him huge sum of money, a luxury car, a bungalow, and several open sites as gift. Pramanik never demanded it but was happy. The dowry helped him to plan a lavish honeymoon in Switzerland and nearby European countries. The media were quick to highlight this fact, and many of his opponents raised their eyebrows. "He would have surely stashed away some of his black money in those Swiss banks. Honeymoon was only an excuse," they alleged.

Mangala gave birth to two beautiful girls in the next four years. She was contended with it and decided not to bear any more child. He wanted a male child for which Mangala wasn't ready. A dejected Pramanik began isolating himself from Mangala. A secret affair with his neighbor Ranjana blossomed.

The widowed Ranjana stayed with her nephew, Arjun, in her big mansion. Arjun's parents were dead in an accident, and since then he was a part of her life. During one of their intimate sessions, Arjun walked into the room. The unexpected sight of his aunt in a tight embrace with Pramanik shocked the boy. In those moments of pleasure, they both failed to notice him. Walking out of the room, the boy headed straight to Mangala and narrated the entire scene. Mangala had devoted her entire life for Pramanik but not anymore, there was no way she could tolerate it. She decided to divorce him, and this made even bigger headlines than their marriage. The news of him being involved in an extra-marital affair also cost him the youth party president's post and nearly ended his career as a politician. Even though Mangala deserted him along with their daughters, Ranjana never gave up. She forced him to marry her. He would have readily agreed to such a proposal had she not insisted on adopting Arjun after their marriage. Ranjana was deeply attached to Arjun; she treated him like her own son. Pramanik rejected the proposal and severed ties with Ranjana as he considered her insensitive to his feelings. Adopting the same fool who cost him his marriage and career was unthinkable. But she wouldn't leave Pramanik so easily. On one or the other pretext, she sent Arjun to his home with a hope that he would start liking the sweet little boy.

Sidelined by both his party and family, Pramanik spent a secluded life at his home. The number of public sightings decreased drastically. Also, the public visits to his house saw a dramatic downfall. The party leadership inducted Mangala into the party, and she became the new voice of the women in the party. In her newly found love for the women's cause and anger towards her ex-husband, she exposed how Pramanik had received an enormous dowry from her father and forced her to bear another baby, hoping it to be a male. If she became third time pregnant, he would have ensured that she underwent a sex determination test. He would have also ensured that she aborted the fetus if it were female, she alleged. If this could happen to her, it could happen to any other woman in the country. "Such evil men should be taught a lesson," she said in her famous speech after joining the party. Taint of dowry, extra-marital affair, amassing large wealth, and alleged female feticide had made him synonymous with every possible social evil that plagued the society.

Every possible worst thing that could happen to a person had already happened with him, he thought. He was devastated and shattered. The good thing about him was that he hadn't turned alcoholic and preferred coffee instead. He didn't want people to attach another tag of a 'drunkard' with him. He still had hopes of making amends and getting his life back on track.

His head ached with the thoughts of his tainted reputation once the boy had left. He returned to the dining table expecting to sip the coffee which he brewed. The cup was empty. He was enraged at the little boy. There was again a knock at the door. He would surely kill the bastard this time and complete the half done job. He darted towards the door and opened it. There stood, Ranjana and Arjun.

"Uncle I forgot to say thank you for that tasty coffee and milk packet," he said sweetly. Pramanik fumed.

"As far as I am concerned our relation is over. I will sue you for child sexual abuse! Hope to see you in court soon," said Ranjana. Arjun innocently pointed at his red cheeks and swollen lips.

THE END

THE LIAR

The first & the last day of college are always memorable. The first day brings with it anxiety, excitement of being in a new atmosphere & meeting new people, desire to scale new heights, and a sense of independence (There is always room for exploring new things). The last day brings with it multitude of mixed feelings like joy of completing the course, at the same time sorrow of separation from friends, and a sense of responsibility.

I still remember the first day of my PG degree course. I was extremely anxious as I climbed the stairs to the second floor of the computer science complex. I had preferred computer networks as my area of specialization for the PG course, in contrast to my electronics background during under graduation, which added to my anxiety. At the same time, I was excited to have joined one of the prestigious Colleges in Karnataka and was determined to do well. I reached the corridors of the second floor. The classes were scheduled to start at 9 A.M., and my watch indicated that I was an hour early.

"The first three hours would be lab sessions," I said to myself on reading the time table on the notice board. The thought of writing programs in computer languages like C, Java, and C++ made me further anxious. My other worry was the HOD of the department.

The inputs I received from the seniors regarding him were not encouraging either. "He is a dangerous 55 year old maniac!" they said. He couldn't dominate his wife at home so went around bossing his staff and students. I even had information that his daughter had enrolled for the course and would be joining our batch. She was the university topper. I had neither seen him nor his daughter but was eager to meet the deadly duo. A beautiful girl joined me after a few minutes. The blue kurta and the black jeans she wore complemented her fair skin and made her look amazing. We greeted each other.

"I am Shoni," she said.

"Nice name. I am Bablu," I said. It was my pet name.

"Very funny!" she smiled. Bablu is as serious a name as Shoni, I thought.

We discussed our educational background. She had completed her under graduation (UG) from the same college and was a topper all throughout her career. I automatically reminded myself that I was from electronics background, for at least the tenth time that morning. 'Hitler's daughter tops in every class. Psycho father has turned his rose like daughter into a book worm. Even she is in your batch this time.' These words of one of the seniors echoed in my mind. Was she his daughter? I was yet to find out.

"You know, the HOD is very strict!" she said. Why was she so interested in discussing him? 'The pleasant morning weather, her hobbies, my hobbies, and the news headlines' she could have discussed anything instead she chose to discuss her father. My sixth sense predicted that she was, in fact, the tyrant's daughter. She was more beautiful than a rose. I decided to impress her using her father as a tool.

"Even my father is strict, yet I love and respect him," I said. I wondered if I had overreacted. "Even if you remain absent for one class, he will suspend you for the entire week that's how strict he is," an enlightened senior had scared me.

"So you are gonna love and respect the HOD? Hee hee," she smiled.

"You know he made me repeat my academic seminar five times, greedy for that one perfect shot," she continued.

She was not going to leave me so easily. But I was determined not to say anything against her father. Which father would torture his fairy like daughter so much? Making her repeat the same boring seminar five times! Such cruel people should be transported to the moon. No. Not moon. They will find their way back; many people have successfully done that in the past. Which is the farthest planet from earth?

"I knew that actor Aamir khan was the only perfectionist in India. It gives me immense joy to know that our HOD is the other one," I said with an exaggerated excitement in my voice. I had not praised so much any living or non living entity anytime, in my life ever. I felt guilty. Guilty of not speaking truth to one of the most beautiful girl I had ever met.

"I have never met such an optimistic and interesting character like you. I don't expect any sympathies, but you could have at least praised my efforts!" she said.

"Would you have delivered the seminar five times without his constant motivation?" I said in my effort to sound extra smart. It wasn't motivation but sheer madness, to be frank.

"You seem to be a big fan of his," she said.

"Well, he was one of the main reasons behind me taking admission here," I declared. Had I known about him earlier then I wouldn't have even admitted myself in the neighboring college, that's how nervous his thought made me in reality.

"I find him strange, and you are just bizarre," she said with a smile. He was definitely strange, but she considered me bizarre? How was bizarre different from strange? Was it a more aggressive form of being strange? Did she consider me to be a lunatic? Had I not praised her father more than anyone else ever?

"Are you not proud of your father?" I asked.

"Yes I am. But why this question suddenly?"

Before she could answer, another girl joined us. She was well fed and resembled an over sized cauliflower.

"Hey Pooja, this guy is a big fan of your dad!" said Shoni without wasting any time.

I was speechless. I felt as if there would be an earthquake, and I would fall effortlessly from the second floor of the building. How wrong I was in guessing that Shoni was the HOD's daughter. The result being she now believed that I was a lunatic. One of my B.E professors always said, "Sixth sense is nonsense!"

"Psycho father has turned his rose like daughter into a book worm," these words of the senior further echoed in my mind. Neither was she a rose nor a worm. She was much larger in size than anticipated.

Three guys joined us in another few minutes. I remained silent, waiting for my chance to meet Shoni alone and clarify that I wasn't a great fan of the HOD. I too strongly condemned his oppressive and tyrant behavior. I wanted to be honest and tell her that I lied. After all the root of every relation is honesty. But I didn't see any realistic chance of that happening as the peon accompanied by the lab instructor opened the doors of the lab. Time had passed rather quickly. It was 8:50 A.M. ten students had gathered inside the lab. We introduced ourselves. Vijay was from my native and from computer science background, this provided some relief. I could rely on someone in case I had doubts during the lab sessions.

The room was filled with chatter as everyone was busy knowing each other's background. Everyone was at ease and occupied a computer next to them as instructed by the lab instructor. The lab had more than 50 computers placed serially at every corner. Shoni was at one of the extreme corners. I was at the other extreme. The fact that she considered me a lunatic was still driving me crazy. I switched on the monitor and the CPU and was busy going through the random images saved in it. Several pictures of famous Bollywood heroines were visible. Rani looked pretty. I was busy in appreciating each of her pictures, when someone placed his palm on my shoulder. I closed the screen in panic.

"Hello young man!" I heard him say. I turned around to notice a gray-haired bespectacled man. He was staring at me with a weird smile on his face.

"Hi," I said naively. I should have said *good morning sir or sorry sir.*

"So this is what I find my students doing on the very first day of their college?" he asked. The best way to respond to such a situation is by remaining silent and behaving as if you have a short term memory loss. I did exactly that.

"What were you doing?" he screamed at the top of his voice. The entire lab was taken over by a weird silence. I felt as if all the others in that room had dropped dead suddenly and turned into zombies. Everyone was staring in my direction. Yes, everyone, including Shoni. The tyrant had finally arrived.

I had to answer something, this time at least.

"Sir, I was typing a program for bubble sort. Suddenly those pictures popped up," I pleaded innocence. That was one of the stupidest things to say, which I soon realized why.

"I seeeeeee," he said. This extra Es made me further anxious.

"Show me the program," he said. Sometimes panic can lead to disaster, and exactly the same had happened. It was barely 30 minutes since I had entered the lab and we had not even received the lab manual or the list of programs. I was sure that others were staring at some picture or the other when they switched on the computer. Even the girls were enjoying seeing their favorite actor's photos. I was sure. But unluckily, I was the one to be caught. It always happened with me.

"Sir, it was here only!" I said and started opening different folders on the desktop. My hurried quest led to more pictures opening up on the screen than before. This time it was Katrina and Aishwarya Rai.

"What nonsense!" he screamed. I looked for a suitable place, to hide myself. I would have unmistakably entered the computer and hid myself, by transforming into a picture, had I belonged to the Harry Potter clan.

"I will throw you out of here!" he said.

Please do it quickly I would be glad, my mind said. It was the first day, and I felt as if someone had stripped me to the last shred of cloth in front of my prospective friends and girlfriend. I glanced through the hall quickly and noticed that Shoni had partially immersed her face in a kerchief. She wasn't crying for me, for sure. The same person whom I had praised so much that morning was hell bent on stripping me in public. Everybody else resembled a zombie. I remained silent.

He stared at me for a few seconds and then cooled a bit. He then inquired about my UG course, my marks, and my family. Was he interviewing a prospective groom for his daughter? He cautioned me that he would keep a close watch on me, and I would have to report to his office when required. I was glad that my nightmare had finally come to an end. He instructed everyone to assemble at the desk and then gave an hour long lecture on the course and college. I was the last one to leave the lab at the end of the session. Everyone including the lab instructor sympathized with me. Shoni was waiting in the corridor and approached me as I was leaving.

"I felt so sorry for you, but I am sure that it was a fruitful learning experience," she said rather sarcastically.

"Rubbing salt on my wounds?" I asked.

"Well, I was just curious to know what exactly made him scream," she said.

"Maybe I didn't greet him and ignored his presence," I said humbly.

"It's not that. It's something else!" she said mischievously as if she believed I was watching porn on the system and was caught red handed.

"He just wanted to scare you people, and for that he chose me. I am lucky. I see that he was successful to an extent possible," I said.

"You know something?" she said.

"I don't know!"

"You are a biiiiiggg liar!"

"Really!"

"I swear by the HOD."

THE END

THE ANONYMOUS
DONOR

The devotees of Murarinagar needed an outlet for their devotion. It was a locality in the budding city of Bidar in Karnataka. Kanha Agarwal, popularly known as the real estate shark, had magnanimously donated the land for the temple. Kanha was his parents' only child. His father Ratanlal possessed acres of land in Kanha's name. The property ran into crores.

Initially, the proposal was to renovate the existing Shiva temple. This was proposed by Shri. Shambhonath Bharadwaj. He was a Brahmin priest of the decades old Shiva temple in the locality. The old temple was in a precarious condition. Its walls were leaky, and the structure was in an urgent need of repair. Patches of fungus and weeds had developed on its outer walls. Shambhonath was in his seventies. The area was dominated by mainly Marwaris, and Gujaratis known for their devotion for Lord Shri. Krishna. Kanha planned to begin his political career by contesting for the councilor elections from the area. Shambhonath led a delegation to the aspiring councilor's house. Kanha understood the need to repair the Shiva temple. The idea of wooing the voters by investing in a temple excited him. It would be a wonderful beginning to his career. But there was a slight change in strategy. A meeting of the well known faces of the locality was called by Kanha. Shambhonath wasn't invited. The bloody history associated with him and the temple was still fresh in memories of the oldest residents of the area. It acted against him.

Kanha proposed to build a Krishna temple in the vicinity. He would make sure that all the hurdles would be cleared. He would also donate a 1000 sq. feet for the purpose. The voters especially the ladies were thrilled to hear the news. Shambhonath resented the turn of events. The destroyer, Shiva, could not be allowed to reside in a ruined structure. A delegation of Shiva devotees led by him failed to convince Kanha. Kanha always carefully weighed the pros and cons of any proposal. Life was a business for him. A life of simplicity and righteousness would earn no dividends. Shambhonath had been a Shiva devotee since time immemorial; he was the caretaker of the temple. He led a life of simplicity and honesty. Everyone in the locality knew him. A number of devotees visited the temple, yet he found it difficult to get the temple restored. He had to beg for favor from others. Shiva had not done him a single favor. He had no property and lived a bachelor's life. He begged for food or performed Vedic rituals in others homes and earned his bread & butter. He stayed in a depleted tiny three room structure in a corner of the ruined temple complex. Kanha believed that the old man was scared for his own safety in case the structure was to collapse one day. Shambhonath was an epitome of an incompetent & failed individual as far as Kanha was concerned. Kanha concluded that investing in a Shiva temple was not a clever idea. It wouldn't guarantee him a victory. But investment in a Krishna temple would ensure that. He believed in no damn god. And more than anything else, he disliked Shiva.

Pandit Pushkarnath was a famous Shiva devotee and had established a Shiva temple on his private 1500 sq. feet area during 1940s. A small three room building in a corner was his dwelling place. He had three sons. The eldest, Shamhbonath, was obedient and humble. The second one, Brahmendra, was power seeker and short tempered. Srinath, the youngest, was rebellious, ill mannered, and greedy. He would never respect anyone, not even Shiva. A number of devotees visited the temple every day. The offerings (money, rice, wheat and sorghum sacks, garlands made of colorful flowers) were an everyday routine. The family accumulated immense wealth in a short span of time. Pushkarnath formed a trust consisting of family members. Wealth brought the tussle over the complete control of the temple. Brahmendra's temper and Srinath's rebellious nature conflicted with each other. A cold war broke out and quickly turned into an ugly spat. It was in 1960s that Pushkarnath died after a long illness. The elder Shambhonath tried his best to convince his brothers and bring about a truce but failed. He even proposed that the devotee's offerings be divided equally between the two, but they rejected it.

Srinath had taken to playing cards and drinking alcohol. Once he performed the evening arati ritual in the temple in a drunken state and abused Brahmendra. The enraged Brahmendra killed him with a machete inside the temple in full view of the devotees. He was jailed. Shambhonath was the sole caretaker. He decided to remain a bachelor all his life. What if his kids repeated the same? He also eliminated the cause that led to conflict between the two brothers. The hundi (a box in which money is offered by devotees) was also removed. No offerings other than flowers were allowed. The ugly episode had caused a bad name for his family and community. People believed that Shiva had cursed the family. Over a period of time, the Smarthas (the Shiva devotees) left the place for greener pastures and only a handful of them remained. But they were in the minority in the area and more importantly they were poor. Their only means of income was by performing pooja in nearby homes during festivals. Shambhonath had an uphill task of setting things right. And bring back the lost glory of the Shiva temple. But it would take some time, maybe an entire lifetime. Shambhonath had to wait.

Kanha's proposal was accepted. The locality members built a grand Krishna temple at a whopping cost of 30 lakh rupees, just 200 meters away from the old Shiva temple. An artistically sculpted beautiful statue of Krishna and Radha was installed in the sanctum sanctorum. The females of the locality organized bhajan on a daily basis. A young Brahmin, Dattu Maharaj, was appointed the priest of the Krishna temple. Kanha became a first time councilor. Just giving away a 1000 sq. feet land in turn gave his career a big breakthrough. At the entrance of the temple, a huge board was hung which read: The

Krishna temple Murarinagar, erected and maintained by the Agarwal charitable trust. A list of the trustees followed it. Kanha's was the first name as he was the trust's president. Inside the temple, two prominent donor's information was displayed in huge font on top of the sanctum door: 1. the land and the Krishna statue donated by Mr. Kanha Agarwal, a great Krishna devotee & 2. Radha statue—donated by Gulabchand Mittal, a textile businessman. Every time Kanha visited the temple, his focus naturally shifted on the letters inscribed above the sanctum door. He derived great pleasure from it and his chest swelled with pride, only then would his eyesight fall on the lord's statue. The ceiling of the temple was full of paintings depicting Krishna's childhood and his dance with the gopikas. Kanha wanted his contribution highlighted everywhere in the temple. Thus, even the face of Krishna in the paintings closely resembled his.

Radha grew up to be a great devotee of lord Shiva. She loved playing with mud as a child. Once it so happened that she started preparing a structure out of clay, and it resembled a Shivalinga. This incident drew her towards Shiva. Her grandma narrated several stories of the supreme god to little Radha, and her fascination for Shiva only increased. You are a great devotee of Shiva, her friends teased. Her grandma being a devotee herself taught Radha many prayers to receive the god's grace. Radha would chant the mantras every day without fail. With every passing day, her devotion only increased by many folds. Her father Hirachand owned a jewelry showroom in the city. He believed that Radha was an incarnation of goddess Laxmi herself. His financial condition had improved, and his business had multiplied since her birth. He fulfilled her every need as his wife had died shortly after Radha's birth. He had decided against a second marriage. His assistant had drawn attention towards the fact that Radha had grown into a beautiful young girl, and the time was ripe for her marriage. This fact made Hirachand nervous. But a girl's true home is her husband's not her father's. He had always taught her to love and respect her husband. It was his only teaching. The search for a groom began and Radha found a soul mate in Kanha. The city witnessed a grand wedding between the two giants of the city. All newspapers splashed the headlines, unaware that very soon they would also be reporting the rumors related to their divorce.

Kanha was happy to have been blessed with such a beautiful wife. She fulfilled all the responsibilities expected of a wife. He took pride in showcasing her qualities in front of relatives and friends. He liked everything about her except one thing, her devotion for Shiva. She would spend hours together chanting mantras, singing bhajans, and performing pooja. She made it a point to visit the age old Shiva temple near their house and got acquainted with Shambhonath. He liked the new devotee and treated her like his own daughter.

"Being Radha, you should devote more time for Kanha and not Shiva," Kanha would tell her.

"Are you jealous of him?" she would say, "You are the most important person in my life only next to Shiva." She even sang bhajans when in a romantic mood, which instantly put off Kanha. The name Shiva appeared in their daily routine several times. She considered lovemaking a divine act, which put him off. He considered sex to be a pleasure and wanted it to be wild. This led to displeasure in their married life. He started staying away from her. As time progressed, he considered Shiva to be his enemy. How could she bear a child if things continued this way? He disliked being the second most important person in her life. Whenever someone uttered Shiva, his facial muscles would contract, and a troubled expression appeared on his face.

"You should have been born 100 years ago. You don't belong to this era," he told her. She ignored his taunts and never disrespected him. The other thing which irritated Kanha was that she had only once visited the brand new Krishna temple built by him, and never stepped into it again. When all the females in the locality were behaving like gopikas owing to the new temple, Radha maintained a distance from it. What was she trying to prove?

"I've decided to rename you as Parvathi. You are not fit to be known as Radha," he mocked her. She maintained silence, and this irritated him further. He kept himself busy in politics. Days turned into months and then years. Their three year old wedding was on rocks. It needed divine intervention.

Radha gave birth to a beautiful baby boy in the fourth year. Kanha considered it an accident. Radha considered it Shiva's grace. The new born had brought their marriage alive. The heir apparent had arrived. The family members were happy that good sense had prevailed, and they both had reconciled. Kanha was happy, but resented the fact that he was now the third most important person in Radha's life. She might take their son along to the Shiva temple, he thought.

Kanha would never tolerate his son being influenced by Shambhonath. The vision of the little Kanha singing songs in praise of Shiva gave him nightmares.

"How much you like hurting me by visiting the ruined temple, and never setting foot in the grand Krishna temple!"

"Oh dear, it's not intentional. If you don't like, then I won't visit. But I would not set foot in the Krishna temple unless you change certain things."

"I am glad that you agreed so easily. It makes me immensely happy that, you've decided not to visit the Shiva temple and not to irritate me. I just can't believe what I've heard. But I don't understand the logic behind staying away from my temple."

"Oh dear, didn't you observe? The Krishna temple suffocates. The temple is a reflection of your pride and ego. It's not about Krishna, it's only about you."

"So what, I made it a possibility. Without me, the temple wouldn't have been a reality."

"Dear, try to understand."

"You do it purposely to hurt me," he said.

'O lord Shiva, the destroyer. Please destroy my husband's ego' she prayed silently.

"But your decision of not visiting the Shiva temple has made me happy. I feel so relieved," he continued.

"Shiva resides in every cell of my body," she said silently. The ignorance of her husband was painful.

"You would visit my Krishna temple from today. Nothing changes in that temple!" he declared with a wicked smile. She remained silent.

Sonu was liked by everyone in the locality. The four year old was a new member of the cricket team in the locality. The kids in the age group of 4 to 10 had formed a team of their own, and regularly played cricket on the main road of the locality. Just adjacent to the road stood the ruined complex of the Shiva temple, and the ball often entered the complex. The cricket match was an obstruction for the plying vehicles. But no one dared to reprimand the kids of the rich parents, especially Sonu Kanha Agarwal the son of the new city MLA. Sonu entered the complex many times while fielding. Sambhonath sat idly in a corner watching the match. Little Sonu just stared at him and left. He never dared go near the old man. Kanha had warned him against venturing near or interacting with Shambhonath. The old man was branded as the child thief, to keep his son away. Shambhonath volunteered to throw the ball into their playground, the main road, several times. His smiling face presented him as a harmless person, yet the kids stayed away. He also protected the kids from the moving vehicles by alarming them whenever a speeding vehicle neared. His dream of renovating the temple was yet to be fulfilled. Three attempts in the last three years to renovate the temple complex were thwarted, by a powerful Kanha.

Kanha would convince the donors to invest their money in the Krishna temple, which had grown in grandeur. If the people disagreed then Kanha would use force, his dislike for Shiva had grown deeper. The MLA had a team of goons at his disposal to scare his detractors. His property had also grown tremendously once he had entered the assembly. Renovating the temple was Shambhonath's only purpose in life now. He was already nearing eighty. His failing health helped him little in his endeavor. The guilt of having failed in repairing the abode of the lord made him restless. He didn't want to die before completing the task. Was Shiva listening?

Once Kanha had to visit Bangalore for an assembly session, his political career kept him busy & away from his native for a number of days. During that time, an anonymous donor had parceled an envelope. It consisted of a twenty lakh cheque along with a letter for Shambhonath. The letter clearly stated that, the money be strictly used for the renovation of the Shiva temple. Incidentally, it was also Mahashivaratri that night. He knew that finally Shiva had heard him. His happiness knew no bounds. He never bothered to verify the identity of the donor. The temple received a tremendous facelift. The newly constructed temple complex was inaugurated by Shambhonath by distributing free meals, using all his savings, as prasadam. On his return, Kanha was furious. His sources informed that it was funded by an anonymous person. It is an era of advertisement and publicity; people don't even feed a beggar unless they have a selfish motive. Remaining anonymous and spending lakhs together on a ruined temple was just unthinkable for Kanha. Who would waste their money on the temple for nothing? He definitely would find out the person and even Shiva wouldn't be able to save the donor. The donor committed blasphemy. Who was the greatest Shiva devotee in their locality? Radha! Definitely the old bastard would have brain washed, and tricked Radha into donating the amount required for renovation. He had no idea about the exact amount that was siphoned off from her and in what way. The shrewd Shambhonath ought to be taught a lesson.

Kanha decided to visit the temple once in the hope of finding a clue to the donor's identity. It was around

8 P.M. He wanted to make sure that Shambhonath had received a fair trial before he received justice at the hands of his goons. The interiority of the temple was mesmerizing and caught instant attention; the grandeur was of a far superior quality than the Krishna temple. Various avatars of Shiva like the Nataraja, Rishabha, and Chandrashekhar among others and the twelve jyotirlingas were carved on the walls. The Shivlingas were gold plated. But there was no mention of any donor(s) anywhere in the temple complex. He searched every nook and corner of the temple complex in the hope of finding one. Shambhonath was busy singing devotional songs, lost in his own world. He seemed to be unaware of Kanha's presence. He would remain in that state for a few hours. Kanha waited for the old man's trance to end.

"Finally you get what you wanted!" Kanha said.

"Welcome to Shiva's abode Kanhaji!"

"I am least interested in chatting and wasting time with you here. Tell me what I want," he said arrogantly.

"What is it?" Shambhonath asked politely.

"Who contributed the money for this?"

"It's all Shiva's grace."

"Come on, you think I would believe your story?"

"It's the truth."

"Are you not interested in having your limbs intact?"

"Nothing scares me now," he said with a smile.

"You bastard tricked my wife into donating such huge money!"

"She would never do anything to displease you."

"You know her better than me? You old rogue?"

"This place is holy; please refrain from using abusive language."

"Son of a bitch, how dare you warn me like that?" said Kanha and punched the old man. The massive blow landed on his jaw and blood oozed out of his mouth. Shambhonath fell on the ground.

"I give you time till tomorrow evening. Be ready to face the consequences after that," he warned and left. His anger had taken the form of a hurricane, and in a fit of rage he lambasted Radha for her unpardonable act. He used the filthiest of abuses against her. She just kept on repeating 'I don't know'.

He waited till the next evening for Shambhonath's confession, and then ordered his goons to thrash the old man mercilessly. Ten minutes later one of the goons came rushing. Shambhonath was dead.

Kanha was dumbstruck. The idiots weren't meant to murder him. They only had to break his limbs and teach him a lesson.

"You scoundrel, senseless being . . . ." he said. The goon interrupted him before he could complete the sentence.

"Sahib, he died while saving your son," he said. Kanha rushed towards the exit and stopped only at the accident spot. A scared Sonu was in Radha's arms. She was consoling him.

"Shambho uncle saved Sonu from a speeding truck. He was fielding at the intersecting curve of the roads," said one of the boys. "Sonu is lucky!" said the other. Shambhonath's still body was lying in a pool of blood. The truck had sped away. His face was serene and calm. Kanha was filled with guilt at the sight. Only last night had he dealt a severe blow on the old man's face, and he had let goons teach Shambho a lesson. He made sure that Shambhonath received a perfect funeral according to his community's customary traditions. He lit the funeral pyre. A man who gave his life to save someone else's son couldn't be ordinary. Tremendous respect roused in Kanha's heart for Shambhonath. He would have to live with a sense of guilt for the rest of his life. The old Shiva temple was now under government's control.

Soon after the incident, the District Commissioner banned the boys from playing on the road. The documents related to the construction plan of the locality revealed that, the Krishna temple stood exactly where a play ground and park were meant to be. The land was illegally acquired by Ratanlal, Kanha's father. The DC, who was an arrogant and honest officer, ordered the demolition of the temple. The Krishna and Radha statues were shifted to new premises. The job was done overnight without taking the residents into confidence and by force. Even the might of Kanha failed to save the grand structure. He served three nights in jail for threatening the DC. His goons were booked under the Goondas Act and jailed for a much longer duration. Ramesh Mittal, an experienced business tycoon, bailed out the goons. He was their new boss. He promised the residents that the Krishna temple would be restored in its original place. He was the new messiah of the residents. Kanha lost the following elections. The statues of Krishna and Radha found a new abode in one of the corners of the renovated Shiva temple. The temple was back to its lost glory. Dattu Maharaj was the temple's new caretaker.

Radha's prayers finally bore fruit. Shiva had destroyed the structure that was an epitome of Kanha's ego.

"Namah Shivay Aum Namah Shivay, Hara Hara Bole Namah Shivay . . . ." was being played at the Shiva temple. Dattu Maharaj was performing the evening arati. Sonu took two steps towards the exit in a bid to escape. He wanted to join his friends in the newly built play ground. Kanha held him back and gestured him to remain silent. Radha smiled. It was the happiest day of her life. It was their first time together in the temple. They were soaked in the atmosphere of devotion. "Namah Shivay Aum Namah Shivay, Hara Hara Bole Namah Shivay . . . ." they sang intensely along with the other devotees. Kanha had ill treated Shambhonath all his life. He had thwarted several attempts by the old man to renovate the temple. He considered him good for nothing. But the old man had done something worthwhile in death. Kanha would be indebted to him all his life.

"You have done a fabulous service by secretly donating the money for renovation. Shambhonath's wish was fulfilled because of us," he told her while heading back.

"It wasn't because of me or us. It's all because of Shiva's grace."

"No point maintaining secrecy anymore. I know it's you."

"It can be anyone but not me," she said.

"You and your devotion are really difficult to understand," he said.

"O lord Shiva, let better sense prevail in my husband," she prayed as they headed for the Krishna temple which was earlier Shambhonath's home in a corner of the temple complex. Radha bowed before the lord.

"What a beautiful sculpture. The sculptor has done a fine job," she commented.

"I guess lord Krishna was more charming than the idol!" Kanha said as they joined a group of devotees in chanting bhajans devoted to the playful Krishna.

On the day of Mahashivaratri:

The aged Don was laid on the hospital bed. He was staring at the face of death. The doctors declared that the dreaded cancer had won the battle. Every bad deed of his haunted him at that moment. Shakeel, his close aide, had not yet arrived with the information that he wanted so desperately. Tracking down Shambhonath was an easy task. But the Don had not gathered the courage to meet Shambho. Shakeel had informed the ailing underworld Don that Shambhonath was in need of money, to renovate the temple. But the Don knew very well that Shambhonath would never accept money from him. He had to remain anonymous. Shakeel had promised him that he would make sure the cheque reached the right hands. But there was no reply yet. Time was fast running out. He found it difficult to breathe. He couldn't hold back any longer. Just then Shakeel arrived with assurance on his face. Brahmendra died peacefully.

THE END

DEEPAK'S SUPERSTITIONS

Never go for shave or haircut on Thursdays, Saturdays, & Sundays. This particular thought echoed in my mind. I looked at the calendar again for the 3rd time and reaffirmed that it was a Thursday indeed, and dropped the idea of a haircut. Apart from this, I had 2 other superstitions. These superstitions developed over a period of time and became a part of my life. My parents, friends, fiancée, prospective in-laws, neighbors, and even the barber were aware of them. Being an engineer, I desperately wanted to weed out the three superstitions in me. But every time I tried, I encountered some or the other problem. It made me desperate & superstitious. The superstitions had soon turned into a belief system.

My grandma always said, "Superstitious people are losers in life. They can never taste success." I recalled this statement when I felt low, but I couldn't overcome them.

I don't pick anybody's calls after 11 P.M. (my 2nd superstition). It once happened that I was sleeping at home, and one of my friends, Kamal called up. He needed help badly as his ATM card wasn't working, and he had run out of cash. He was in a pub at that time and was fully drunk. I rushed to his help with 2000 rupees. When I reached the place, I found that he had picked up a brawl with the pub manager for alleged mistreatment meted out to him, in spite of him being a regular customer. The manager was in no mood, to relent. His goons had beaten Kamal badly. When I protested, they beat me up too while snatching all the cash and damaging my bike.

"DEJAVU's doors are closed forever for beggars like you," the manager, in turn, insulted us. "Don't ever dare come even near our pub," he warned.

"You bastard, we are free citizens. Who are you to stop us?" Kamal thundered. "I will definitely take revenge. Wait and watch!" Kamal was the son of a millionaire, but his drinking habit made him unpopular among his family members. He uttered a lot of things in the drunken state, which made little sense at that time. He was abusive. I took him to the nearest hospital.

When he came back to senses, he couldn't see me eye to eye. He felt guilty for having dragged me into it for no reason and apologized. The guilt was so strong, in spite of my best efforts, we lost contact thereafter.

On another occasion, I received a call close to 12 A.M. by another friend. He and his girl friend had planned to get married, and they needed a place to hide for the rest of the night. I decided to help them. God only knew how his father came to know about it and landed at my room after an hour, and created a ruckus.

I had to vacate the room when my house owner termed me a nuisance. But nothing wrong has happened with calls that I received before 11 P.M.

My phone rang at around 11:30 P.M on a Friday; I decided not to pick it. My superstition wouldn't let me receive the call. It rang again. It was from an unknown number. I didn't pick it again. The phone just continued to ring. I put it in silent mode and kept it under the pillow. After half an hour when I checked it, there were around 20 missed calls from the same unknown number. It made me curious and worried. What if someone were genuinely in need? What if it were a question of life and death for one of my friends? I recalled what grandma always said. I had to overcome my superstition this time.

I received the call finally, and it was just the beginning of the troubles that lay ahead.

"Have you gone deaf?" asked the female voice.

"Who's this?"

"This is your grandma."

"Sorry!"

"You don't recognize your grandma's voice? Idiot!" she said.

I knew for sure that she was playing a prank. My grandma couldn't have called from heaven.

"Ma'am kindly let me know your actual identity. This suspense is too much to handle."

"Deepak idiot can't you identify my voice? I am Sanjana!" I simply couldn't believe it. She was my close friend in school, but after that we had lost contact. It was a pleasant surprise.

"I can't believe it. Are you the same Sanjana who had stolen my Tiffin in the school, and left me crying the entire day?"

"Yeah and this happened several times," she said.

"Glad to hear from you after so long."

"Let's meet tomorrow, there is a surprise in the waiting," she said. We spoke for half an hour, but she never told me how she got my number. I promised her to meet the next day sharp at 9:00 A.M. I was so excited the entire night that I slept very late and little.

I woke up at 8:30 A.M the next day and in a hurry left for the saloon. The constant work pressure provided very little time for other stuff. I couldn't have met her with a fully grown beard and shabby hairs. I had to look presentable. I always started the day by staring at lord Krishna's poster pasted on the wall (my 3rd superstition) for five minutes and then went ahead with my daily routine. I had been following the ritual since my early adolescent days. People pray, but I didn't offer any prayers. I just stared at him. It gave me courage. That morning, unfortunately, I forgot to stare at him.

"Just trim my hairs and give a clean shave," I told the barber while seated on the chair.

"Hi young man, surprised to see you here on a Saturday!" I heard someone say. To my disbelief my fiancée, Chaitanya's, father was seated on the chair next to mine. His face was fully covered in foam. I had won a battle of sorts, when I made him believe that, I was the right choice for his daughter. There were many differences between us. My family was pure vegetarian, but they were non-vegetarians. We spoke Hindi at home, and they spoke pure Kannada. I had a job in IT Company, but they wanted a businessman for their daughter. Yet I succeeded in convincing him. Especially, the cops are difficult to convince. He is a traffic cop. I consider it one of the biggest achievements of my life.

"Dad, I have some urgent office work today," I lied. If only he came to know that I had broken my superstition for a girl, he definitely would take it in a wrong sense. So I decided to keep things simple. I even hid it from my fiancée; even she would not tolerate me breaking my superstitions, just to look presentable for a girl other than her. There was no need for me to look presentable before any other girl since she had entered my life, she believed. I was acceptable to her in any shabby look. "Looks don't determine one's true character," she always said. Other girls shouldn't matter to me anymore. My looks shouldn't matter to them.

"See how dedicated is my son-in-law. His work is more important to him than his superstitions," he said to the barber proudly. I just smiled. Nothing had gone wrong so far. I parked my two-wheeler in a lane adjacent to the main road and arrived at the cool joint spot at Jayanagar in Bangalore, the place where I was supposed to meet Sanjana. I was already late by one hour. She made me wait for 30 minutes more.

"Hi hero!" she greeted upon arrival. I simply couldn't believe my eyes. I had never imagined that I would see her again. She had grown into a beautiful young lady.

"Hi Sanju!" we hugged each other.

"I am really very hungry. I want to eat pani puri!" she said sweetly.

"Hey! Let's have a soup and then eat burger followed by a juice," I told her.

"No dude, pani puri is my favorite and this guy is a specialist in it. Come na."

"Actually I have an allergy from pani puris."

"Allergic to pani puris! I have never heard such a thing before."

"I mean I don't like its taste; also it's early morning. Let's have some healthy breakfast."

"Oh come on! You haven't changed a bit in all these years. This is our first meeting after a long time; let us celebrate it through pani puris. There can't be a better way than that." I never understood why girls are so crazy after the unhygienic, road side junk food.

"Yeah you eat PP, and I will celebrate using cold and delicious mango shake."

But she was not the one to leave so easily. She always had the habit of doing & saying peculiar things. I could never imagine eating junk food for breakfast.

She ordered one plate and ensured that I tasted at least one while she praised the vendor for the taste. We discussed childhood things and things related to our past, like how we lost contact and what happened thereafter. She had gone to U.S. for higher studies and returned only recently. We then roamed around in the shopping area, spending quality time together. I hid from her that I was engaged. I decided to reveal it at a later time as surprise. I gifted her watch and she complemented me by presenting a branded T-shirt and jeans. We returned around 1:00 P.M. On our return my bike was missing. I ensured that it was the same place where I had parked it earlier.

"What happened to the bike that was parked here?" I asked a nearby shopkeeper.

"You can only park here on Mondays, Wednesdays, and Fridays. Didn't you see the board?" he said. I then read the sign board carefully.

"Go and get it from the nearest police station," he said.

Sanjana noticed that I was tensed and tried to instill confidence that I would get the bike back safely. She even apologized as it was all her idea. I told her that I wasn't tense, and it wasn't her fault in any way. I was worried about getting my bike back and I knew that it wasn't going to be an easy task. I shouldn't have met her at that spot in the first place; of all the places in Bangalore was it the only place available for us to meet? The answer was a big 'no'.

The police station was at a walk away distance. I couldn't have sent her to inquire about the bike. I had to do it myself.

"Sir, I am the owner of this vehicle," I told the policeman who was seated on my bike with his back facing me.

All hell broke loose when he turned to respond. It was my prospective father-in-law. His face suddenly stiffened as he saw Sanjana standing by my side. Then the unthinkable happened.

"Sir, please return the bike. We have some seriously urgent work," said Sanjana.

"What work?" he asked, raising eyebrows.

"We came here to shop for our marriage. In a hurry, he forgot to check the sign board. We need to visit few other places urgently," she said much to his agony. Only she could have given such a peculiar excuse. I was carrying those shopping bags with me. He was shaken as if a nuclear bomb were dropped on him. I wanted to run for cover. What the hell was she telling?

"Sanjana, what are you talking? There is no need to lie," I said without looking at him.

"Deepak, don't worry. Sir will definitely understand our situation. Here is our marriage card. You are also invited." She took out a marriage card from her purse and gave it to him.

He read it twice and gave a puzzled look. I snatched it from him and to my utter disbelief, whatever she said was true. It was her personal marriage card and the groom's name was also Deepak. But then I wasn't the Deepak mentioned in the card. I had no means to prove this to my prospective father-in-law. It was enough for him to pronounce me guilty.

"You bastard you have ruined my daughter's life!" he said and punched his heavy fist on my right jaw. I lay on the ground the next second. A tiny group of people had assembled around me in no time. Several people were mute spectators to this tragic incident.

Only then did Sanjana realize the gravity of the situation.

"He ruined your daughter's life?"

"This bastard is engaged to my daughter. I will make sure that he spends the rest of his life in Tihar jail," he declared.

"Oh my god it's a blunder!" she said on realizing her mistake. "Wait a minute uncle. It's all, my mistake. He is innocent!"

"No, it's not your mistake. This pampered bastard is playing with two girls' lives at the same time. We don't know how many girls are hidden in his closet!"

"No, no. You are getting me wrong. It was a lie. Give me a chance to explain," she pleaded. He gave a puzzled look.

"When we found that the bike was missing, I thought about an appropriate excuse to gain your sympathy. That's the reason I told you that we were about to get married. Cops usually melt when they hear such romantic excuses. This is one trick, which has saved me and my fiancé once before."

"Then what about the card and his name on it?"

"It is just a coincidence. I was here to give Deepak a surprise. The surprise was that my fiancé's and his name are both the same. I just wanted to play a prank on him by showing him the marriage card, but everything has gone haywire. I and this Deepak whom you punched just now are both school friends. We have met today after a very long time. I am expecting my fiancé any moment here; I've already informed him about the incident," she said in one breath. SMS makes it very easy to share things these days.

"Oh! What a blunder I have committed. Get up son. Are you alright?" he said with a sense of urgency and belonging.

"I got up adjusting my shifted jaw."

"I am alright!" I said angrily.

"Oh what a blunder I have committed! I failed to recognize that it was your bike," he said.

"It's my mistake entirely. I should have told you the truth when we met at the saloon this morning." I cursed myself. Deepak, her fiancé landed near the traffic police station.

"Hi Deepak, let me introduce you to my friend," she said.

We shook hands. "She still remembers you after such a long time," he said. I congratulated them.

Then he turned to my prospective FIL. "So he is the cop who has taken your bike into custody?"

"No, he's my prospective FIL!" I had introduced them before any other tragedy struck.

They then shook hands and greeted each other.

Then Deepak turned to me. "Nice meeting you and I would have loved to spend time with you, but we need to visit a few of our friends and distribute the wedding cards. Sanju shall we leave?"

"Yap, do come along with your fiancée. Here, is your card and please forgive me for this episode," Sanjana said.

"Such things do happen. I am alright. By the way, who gave you my number?"

"Kamal is my cousin. He owns DEJAVU now. He has finally taken his revenge. You should visit him once," she said. I understood that he had narrated her that night's episode. Deepak and Sanjana left for their next destination.

"I need some rest. I shall leave now," I told my FIL. He was extremely apologetic for his behavior.

"A father has all the right to slap." I consoled him and left. It wasn't a slap. It was like a heavy punch on an opponent's face while boxing.

The day had been a letdown so far. There was no electricity at home. The surroundings were extremely silent. I had a sinking feeling. Getting a punch from my FIL in full public view especially in front of my childhood friend was insulting. My head ached, and my heart pained. I had broken the three superstitions and the consequences were before me. Then a certain curiosity developed. What would happen tomorrow? When these beliefs didn't apply to anyone else in the world, why did they only matter to me? Things had gone wrong only because I had parked the bike in the wrong place. Things went wrong because Sanjana had this habit of saying peculiar and weird things, without understanding its consequences. It was just a coincidence that the traffic cop turned out to be my father-in-law. If it were a different person, I wouldn't have received the punch in the first place. The situation was created only because of my actions and others' reactions. For the first time, I had questioned my superstitions. They had turned into strong beliefs. There was no way the same would happen tomorrow in case I again broke them. But something would happen, and I was ready for it.

I waited eagerly for a call after 11 P.M. I expected at least someone to call me. Finally, the phone rang. It was Chaitanya. She apologized on her father's behalf for his massive punch. I told her that I shouldn't have hidden the truth from him. Her father had given a diktat that we shouldn't meet before marriage, and we adhered to it strictly. There was still three months time for our marriage. She said that she personally wanted to meet me the next day and apologize. I said that there was no need for her to apologize, the chapter was already closed. But she didn't relent. It had been 3 months since we last met for our engagement. Seeking apology was just an excuse for her to meet me. She had already apologized on phone. We spoke for nearly two hours and decided to meet in a Chinese restaurant on MG road, in the evening. The next morning, I avoided staring at lord Krishna while heading straight to the barber.

"Welcome sir, it's extremely rare to see you on a Sunday!" he said.

"Yeah, you haven't trimmed my hairs properly," I said and made him trim them again for no fault of his. He gave surprised look but did his job.

I went back home, got ready and eagerly waited for the clock to tick 7 P.M. When I headed for the restaurant my only concern was her father. What if he spotted us together? The busted superstitions were playing on me mentally, making me nervous.

When I reached the hotel, Chaitanya was already waiting. Her charming smile greeted me. We hugged each other and tears of joy trickled down her eyes. Everything was going on perfectly. We ordered a hot & sour soup and roasted chicken leg pieces, her favorite. I explained her in detail the previous day's incident. We had a lot to share. Then the dish arrived. It looked very delicious.

I picked up a leg piece and the next moment I screamed.

"What happened?" she was horrified.

"The jaw hurts!"

She smiled. We spent a wonderful time together. It turned out to be the most memorable day. Just when I was about to sleep, I looked at lord Krishna's poster. He stared at me angrily.

THE END

THE
UNFULFILLED WISH

"We will always be together in life and death,"
they promised each other. But Elena couldn't keep
the promise. She went on her heavenly journey alone.
Though he knew it would happen, the trauma was
unbearable. He felt betrayed and wanted to end his life.
Then he read the note she had left. "Dear, you have
to live. Remember my wish? I know you will fulfill it.
I know how you would feel, once I am gone. But how
can I ever betray my sweet heart? I would continue to
live in your thoughts. Nobody can ever separate us—
Your Elena."

She knew that it would be impossible for him to
live without her, but she wanted him to live on. She
knew very well that he would have definitely fulfilled
her wish. When she was alive, he had strongly rejected
the idea. Now that she had gone, his only motive was
to fulfill her last wish. Her entire life was an epitome
of selflessness. He decided to bury her in the backyard,

where she spent most of her time listening to the chirping of birds and writing poetry. The backyard housed her favorite plants, trees, and a sprawling lush green lawn. She had planted a number of rose plants in the garden. The thorns in the plants reminded her about the reality of her life. The different colored roses reminded how colorful her life had been because of Michael. She suffered from blood cancer and in spite of his best efforts; he had failed to save her life. He along with the neighbors gave her a silent burial. The priest completed the formalities. He erected a white marble slab at the place with the help of others. He would use it to communicate his feelings with her, by writing on it. He spent that whole night near the tiny tomb.

Michael and Elena had spent 30 years of their blissful marriage together. Their only son had never tried to contact them in the past few years. Michael always kept track of him through the internet and felt happy that his kid had learnt to live without them. Their son had a love marriage and his wife succeeded in making him settle in U.S. (away from them). Initially, their son called them frequently. The frequency dropped with time and the calls stopped completely.

The next morning Michael woke up disturbed, but she lay peacefully in the grave. He envied her. He had to complete the task. He prepared a matrimonial ad and headed straight to the offices of some of the popular newspapers. At 75, his chances of finding a bride were highly dismal. The publishers looked at him in disbelief and went ahead with their job. He paid them heavily for publishing his ad on the front page. He even registered online on several matrimonial sites. He wanted this ordeal to complete as early as possible. The very next morning his ad appeared in several newspapers. It read: A widowed man of seventy five looks for a companion. Age and religion have no bar. He owns an independent house with a scenic backyard and a luxury car. He is a retired central government employee. Thirty years of blissful married life drives him to have some more of it. The ad was followed by his address and contact number.

The news spread like wild fire in his locality in Coimbatore, Tamil Nadu. The locality members always believed that he cared and loved Elena a lot. They believed that he was devastated because of her demise. But the morning news devastated them. They just couldn't believe that it was the same Michael they knew for the past twenty odd years.

He spent the entire day near the tomb, telling her about the advertisement and rewriting the ad on the marble. He expressed his love for her and recalled some of their romantic moments. She rested peacefully in the grave. He told her that if at all he found a companion, then that would be the happiest moment of his life, not because he wanted to start his life afresh, but that would mean fulfilling her last wish. But he hated this wait and the torment he was going through. She knew very well that he could never live without her. There was no question of anyone taking her place or replacing her in his life. It was just a last ditch effort from her to provide him a companion. He knew how worried she was in her last days, not because she was dying. She was worried for him and wanted someone to take care of him.

He recalled her last wish several times as he sat beside the grave. "You should find a suitable companion after I am gone. It's my wish!" she had said. Every time she spoke about it, he stopped her midway. He had never let her complete it. "We will always be together in life and death," he made her promise several times, being fully aware of the truth. So she never fully expressed her last wish. As he was recalling it, he suddenly felt rejuvenated. She never said that he should marry someone and stay with her for the rest of his life. She only wanted him to find a suitable companion. If only he found someone suitable, her last wish would be fulfilled. This made him joyous. He experienced mixed emotions throughout the day. She was true; every thought of his was filled with her memory.

In the evening, his friends Roger and Naveen approached him. They were also his immediate neighbors. They supported his decision to remarry, only adding that he was a way too quick. They expressed hope that he might soon find a bride of his liking. They were in a confused state of mind. They didn't know whether to be happy with his decision, to move ahead in life so quickly, or to express their sadness over Elena's death. But for them one thing was clear that he was out of his mind. He uttered more to himself and looked lost in his thoughts. The very next morning he received a call.

"Hello," he said and recognized the person at the other end at once.

"Is that you Adam, my son?" a spark of joy arouse in him on listening to his son's voice. At last his only son had called. He wanted to convey this to Elena immediately by running to her grave, her new abode. How happy she would be on getting this news!

"No relation exists between us, you shameless old man! It's only been a couple of days since she passed away and you are on a look out for a new bride?"

"So you have been keeping track of us? I knew my son would be back one day," he said.

"Just shut up and listen!" the voice thundered. "Now I know how right was Monica (his wife), when she said that you were one hell of a selfish and shameless guy. She understood you rightly and took me away from you intelligently," he said. When Adam had already formed an opinion about him then there was no point in trying to convince, Michael thought. He realized what his son was up to and remained a patient listener. He was grateful to have heard his son's voice after such a long time. The words hit him like nails.

"Speak son, please don't stop. You don't know how thirsty I am to listen to your voice."

"This is just height of shamelessness. I pity you and your age and your dream of marrying again. Just think about your dead wife, you have let her down so badly."

"Go on."

"Feel so shameful to be your son. And listen to me carefully; this is the last time I am talking to you. The more I think about you, the more embarrassed I feel. When I graduated, you didn't want me to leave you people alone, right? You had even created a significant fuss about it. I always felt guilty that I had to go. Now I am a big man. I have made a name for myself in the fashion industry, and to be frank I don't regret my decision anymore. Especially after knowing how selfish you are. If I had listened to you, god knows what would have become of me."

"You don't feel anything for your mother?"

"Was she any different from you?"

"She was just like me," said Michael.

The phone was already disconnected from the other side. He spent the rest of the day at the grave. "Adam still loves us!" he told his beloved wife.

The very next day Michael received calls for alliance. Several prospective brides called him. He interviewed each one of them. Roger and Naveen believed that the old man loved flirting with young ladies over the phone. Their belief spread in the neighborhood. But Elena's words echoed in his mind, "You should find a suitable companion after I am gone. It's my wish." He rejected a majority of the proposals. After a week's delay, he invited a lady named Sarah. She was a divorcee and hailed from a wealthy background. It was time to have a one to one meet.

There was a knock on the door and a thin, neatly dressed, beautiful lady appeared. She was half his age. He welcomed her. She greeted him with a smile and silently took to chair. It was raining heavily, and she was fully wet. She rejected his offer of drying herself with a towel as she liked getting drenched.

"Would you prefer tea or coffee?"

"No formalities please!" she said.

"You might prefer some toasts with cream."

"Why don't we just sit and discuss matters," she said. Even Elena never liked formalities and got straight to work.

"I was curious to know something!" he said.

"Why a young lady like me wants to marry someone much older than her?" she said cleverly.

"Yeah you might find someone far better than me," he said.

"The very next day after your wife's death, you put an ad in the newspaper for a prospective bride.

It strangely interested me. Generally, it gives an impression that you are a stone hearted person or rather someone without emotions." She paused and observed his reaction. He signaled her to continue.

"Your ad also goes on to show how much you loved and valued your thirty year old relationship," she said.

"Ok go ahead."

"Your house and car don't interest me either. I took excellent care in choosing my first husband, and the wedding was a disaster. He was young, dashing, rich, and influential. But he left me for another woman. I was angry. Then I realized that, things don't go your way always. Life goes on."

"Life has taught you so much at such a young age."

"You know what brings me here?" she said ignoring him. "I have this strange and strong feeling that you couldn't have put this ad unless your wife wanted it and I respect that. There can't be a better husband than you." It took him by surprise.

"I wonder what makes you think so!" he said.

"Thirty years of blissful married life drives him to have some more of it, can have different interpretations. But I know what it exactly means!" she said.

His happiness knew no bounds for he had found someone suitable to be his companion. Neither his close friends, nor his own son had understood him. He found himself lucky to have accomplished the motive that kept him going after her death. He had to share this good news with Elena. He had to tell her that her last wish was finally fulfilled. He asked Sarah to wait for him and headed towards the grave. It rained heavily, but he seldom cared. He was ecstatic for he never anticipated that he would fulfill her last wish so early.

The lawn was slippery, but he didn't care and darted towards the tomb in a great hurry. As he approached the grave, he had a giant slip and his head hit the marble of the tomb. Blood oozed out of his head. He lay on the ground motionless, never to rise again. He couldn't tell her that he had, at last, found someone. It remained his unfulfilled last wish.

THE END

THE RIGHT KICK

Nathulal dreamed of making his son a footballer. Being a native of Bengal, football was his craze. Pele, the Brazilian great was his idol. He had even named his son Peleram. Nathulal worked as a driver at the Oberois. The Oberois owned a chain of hotels in Kolkata.

Mr. Oberoi was impressed by Nathulal's dedication. He was the highest paid employee amongst the Oberoi's staff. Peleram grew up watching his father work dedicatedly for his boss. His father sometimes skipped meals, in order to match his boss's demanding schedules. Peleram aka Ram was forced into playing football, during the early days in school by his father. Once he fractured his leg while playing for the school. A hefty opponent hadn't noticed poor Ram while aiming for the goal and kicked his left leg. Ram took complete bed rest for the next one week. At the same time, he decided that he would never play football in his life again. The next time Nathulal forced him to participate in a football game, Ram out rightly rejected it.

He, now, wanted to be a driver like his father. He had seen how Nathulal's utmost dedication and sincerity had made him Oberoi's favorite employee. Ram barely managed to pass every year. As soon as he turned 18, he joined a driving school and learned the art. Nathulal never liked his son's choice of profession. He wanted Ram to fulfill his dream by joining a soccer club. Always better be late than never, he thought. But Ram was sure of getting an easy job at the Oberois. Nathulal soon resigned from the job owing to old age and failing eyesight. Ram grabbed the opportunity with both hands. The very next day he visited Mr. Oberoi and convinced him for a drive. Since the security guards knew Ram's father, they provided him easy access to Mr. Oberoi. Even Oberoi was in need of a good driver and had known Ram since his childhood days. Ram showcased his abilities to the fullest. The drive was smooth like butter. Mr. Oberoi offered him the job which he had aspired for years. Ram believed his father would create obstacles in the path and would again force him to be a footballer. So he decided to keep his visit to Mr. Oberoi a secret. It surprised and shocked Nathulal when his former colleagues reported the matter to him.

Mr. Oberoi had struggled a lot in life to be successful. He valued discipline, punctuality, and cleanliness. A disciplined individual could reach greater heights and no one can stop him from being a leader, he believed. His mantra was that cleanliness was an integral part of one's life, and people who ignore cleanliness can never be termed disciplined. They wouldn't be able to taste success. He would never tolerate untidy individuals around him. His colleagues believed, his eye for cleanliness, was driving him insane. He had fired many of his chefs on spotting a tiny mark of spilled oil or dal on their uniforms. The customers would never again visit the hotels if they find the chefs uniform untidy. 'Cleanliness, Timing, and Taste' was the tagline of his chain of hotels.

Ram was appointed the driver of the same car which his father drove until a few days back. He was made to undergo a probationary period for the first three months. He took care of the white BMW like it was a queen. He would not tolerate anyone getting closer to it other than his boss. Even if the kids littered the car, he would clean it as soon as possible. He thought about the car every second. Mr. Oberoi had given him a big lecture on the importance of time in one's life. He even gifted Ram a costly Titan watch. On one, occasion, Mr. Oberoi discovered a tiny black dot on the bumper and pointed out that it was synonymous with a dreadful black spot, on Ram's driving career. The young Ram dreamt of owning a BMW of his own one day.

"A driver's job is not just driving, but to ensure that he maintains the standards of his boss. Driving a dirty car is like insulting the boss," Oberoi had lectured.

Kids once had littered peanuts inside the car, and Ram was made to search every inch until he had successfully found the last remaining peanut. His salary for that particular month could very well be compared to peanuts. He was the owner of the car in Oberoi's absence.

Ram was treated as a celebrity in his locality. He stayed in a slum whose residents worked for meager salaries. He did his best to please the boss. After every drive, he would clean the car with a specially made woolen cloth. Two years of utmost dedication, cleanliness, and punctuality impressed Mr. Oberoi. He presented Ram with a brand new white dress. "Continue your good work and success undoubtedly would kiss your feet one day," he said. Ram was overwhelmed by his words and responded with enthusiasm. Nathulal just couldn't understand his son's passion for driving. He found it difficult to believe that someone could be successful in life and earn fame, by being a driver. He told his son about how a small town boy, Pele, had made it big in the world of football. "Even you can do the same. The Royal club of Bengal is in need of youngsters like you. Give it a thought," he suggested.

Ram felt irritated by his father's never ending love for Pele and football. His friends called him Pele meaning 'yellow' in Hindi. Ram hated his father for giving him such a name. "Why can't the old man appreciate his son when his former boss was a fan of his son's skills? Was the father jealous because Ram was a better driver than him?" This thought lingered in his mind most of the time. He loved his job more.

One day he drove Mr. Oberoi to a late night party in one of the Hotels. Ram knew that it would last all night long. Oberoi even partied in a disciplined way and drank only as much as he could handle. He maintained strict timings for parties. After dropping Oberoi at the hotel, Ram parked the car in one corner and waited inside it. He felt sleepy for a split second and then heard a violent screech. Panicked by the noise Ram got down the car, to investigate the matter. A group of drunken teenagers had skid past the white BMW leaving a noticeable scratch on the left side.

Anger surged in him like a tsunami wave. His two years of dedication would be a waste if only his boss noticed it. Even though, it wasn't his fault, the boss would surely hold him accountable. The offenders had to be punished. He ran towards the silver colored Innova and abused the driver. The drunken men got down the car and beat Ram black and blue. Ram could have definitely defended himself against two men. But five proved difficult to overpower. One of them hit him with a rod and inflicted grave injury to his hand; another person kicked him in the stomach while the third guy practiced deadly kicks on his face. The other two vented their anger by heading towards the white BMW and breaking its windshield. They also made severe dents on the bonnet.

The security personnel were successful in stopping them, but till then the damage was already done. The miscreants fled the scene leaving a profusely bleeding Ram on the floor gasping for breath, seething with anger at his helplessness. The security personnel then raised an alarm. They finally located its owner. Mr. Oberoi came running out. The sight of his damaged car turned him red. The driver shouldn't have been irresponsible. It was the driver's responsibility to take care of the car, and he had failed miserably. He then turned the attention towards his bleeding driver. Ram's eyes reflected guilt and a feeling of helplessness.

Ram had expected Mr. Oberoi to show a sense of urgency and take him to the nearest hospital quickly. Mr. Oberoi was a good driver himself. He stared at Ram in anger and asked the security to arrange a taxi and take him to the nearest hospital. After a few seconds, he left the scene to rejoin the party. The party was not meant to be over so quickly. It would fetch him a million dollar deal from another business tycoon. It made no sense to leave the party midway for a driver. Oberoi would never use the damaged car again. He wouldn't use the services of the driver too.

The boss's behavior had shocked Ram. Was his blood not clean that he had to be taken to the hospital in a taxi and not the BMW?

Were the basic traits of humanity completely missing in today's rich class? He had almost lost his life in the brawl, and in return, he received a cold stare? His father had served Oberoi throughout his life. Ram had worked day in and day out to meet his boss's expectations and demands. And he received a cold stare? What he needed was sympathy and accolades for fighting five men.

He had been treated like a football by the miscreants. He could not defend himself or the car. Of what use was the job which provided no security and self respect? An ambulance arrived after a few minutes, and the security personnel helped him stand up. A sense of hopelessness had engulfed him. He wanted to cry. In a span of few minutes, he had experienced a series of emotions. He was now being taken away. Just when he was about to enter the ambulance, like a lightning he turned and marched towards the BMW, and kicked it hard. Screaming in pain he fell on the ground. But the kick made him feel good. On the way to the hospital, his mind was occupied by only one thought. He would not let anyone kick him again. Then he thought of his father, Pele, football, and the Royal club of Bengal.

THE END

COMMUNICATION
DISASTERS

Name: Sumit.
Age: 23.
Degree: Computer science and engineering from AIT University, Pune.
Aggregate percentage: 70.
Employed at: Still unemployed.
Strengths: Technically sound.
Weakness: None (though people say I fail to communicate).

The above mentioned information was a part of my detailed resume. In spite of a good percentage, I failed to get a job through campus placements. I always believed that the problem rests with the other side; people with less IQ generally failed to communicate with me.

My parents were worried as the search was getting longer. I tried unsuccessfully in several off campus placement drives held in different parts of Pune. There were fifty of us who hadn't found favor with the companies during the campus placements. We made it a point to keep in touch with each other, and attend the off campus interviews together. I was one of the brightest among the lot, technically. Every time we appeared, for the written tests and group discussions, a handful of us would get through. And finally land with a job offer. I made it to the HR (the last) round on many instances but couldn't clear it.

Seven months had passed without any success. The number of unsuccessful aspirants in our group was now reduced to twelve. All of them had an aggregate percentage of 55 or less. Many others who got a job had lesser aggregate than me. Friends revealed me that other people got through interviews due to the tie up with HR managers, and higher ups in the companies.

"The amount of money you are ready to pay decides your job profile," one friend said. Who knows, people might talk about me the same way when I get a job! I never paid any attention to such distractions and focused on my preparation. I only targeted the multinational companies. I deserved to be in a MNC. Even though, I received several interview calls from low paying local IT companies, I simply ignored them.

Everyone in the Kelkar Enclave (The apartments where we lived) was now aware that a wannabe IT professional continued to exist in their prestigious neighborhood. The seven storey apartments were full of successful people. Success to them meant working in a reputed firm like an ass, earning lakhs together, owning a car, and then getting married to a beautiful lady. I was the only ineligible bachelor in the enclave.

It was a Sunday when a successful young couple occupied the vacant neighboring flat on the 5th floor, the same floor as ours. The very next day, they celebrated their arrival by throwing a dinner party and invited the distinguished neighbors. I was forced to attend it as my parents had been to attend another function. My 7th straight month, without a job, had generated a sense of inferiority. I preferred to stay away from the quizzical eyes of the neighbors. Only rarely was I spotted.

"Welcome," greeted the hostess with a charming smile. This was the first time I had a closer look at her. She was just marvelous, akin to an angel. Anybody couldn't help but notice her beauty.

"You are Sumit, right? Where are uncle and aunty?" she asked. In a day's time, she knew quite a lot which was surprising. She introduced herself as Mrs. Avasthi. I explained the reason for my parents' absence and my unintended presence. Her husband was a heavily built, tall, bespectacled man. He wore a serious look and spoke in a deep voice.

"Welcome," he said in a serious tone. I shook hands with him and entered.

Earlier in the day I had appeared for an interview in a MNC. The HR executive had grilled me a big deal leaving me distraught. But the sight of the charming lady was so refreshing that I felt happy for no genuine reason. The other guests inquired about my whereabouts. "It's very difficult to hire these days. Quality engineers are hard to come by," said Srikanth, a HR executive in a reputed firm. He stayed on the 3rd floor. He only wanted to prove that I lacked the Q (quality) factor in me. Kesar aunty of the ground floor said that I looked thinner, and needed to focus on my health more, rather than a job. She always had a habit of poking nose into matters highly irrelevant to her survival. A few others, too, made some highly forgettable comments. None came forward and motivated. I wanted to go away from there as soon as possible, but the party had just begun. I looked around for something to distract my mind and my gaze stopped at the hostess.

She was busy serving cold drinks to the guests at a distance. 'She is definitely like Genelia in looks. Her eyes are more like Aishwarya,' my mind was busy making its own conclusions. I liked the texture of her hair. They were long, silky, shiny, and straight. She would be selected easily for a shampoo ad. The moment I took my eyes away from her, I found another pair of eyes staring coldly at me. It was her husband. I managed a smile and immediately looked in a direction opposite to his wife.

After a few minutes, she approached me with a tray full of soft drinks. Her charming smile shifted my attention to her lips. A dark pinkish lipstick adorned her otherwise petal like lips. I readily picked one glass.

While she was returning to other guests, I noticed her waist. It wasn't more than 28 inches. I kept looking, possibly to divert my attention from the taunting neighbors. The moment I shifted my attention elsewhere did I run into a pair of red seething eyes. They resembled an erupting volcano. The stare was now much colder. I managed a fading smile. It faded as soon as it appeared. Only god knew since when that monstrous husband of hers was staring at me. I felt terrorized.

In my effort to divert attention, I took out my cell phone and pretended to dial some numbers and type some messages. I also avoided accidentally running into Mr. Avasthi's draconian stares. But I knew for a fact that a pair of evil eyes was constantly keeping a watch on me.

Once back home, I decided to apologize to Mr. Avasthi in the morning for my uncivilized behavior. A jobless good-for-nothing guy like me had no business staring at a beautiful lady like that. If only I had a job, then things could have been different, I thought. My presence at the prestigious party was unwarranted in the first place. Mr. Avasthi would have been informed well in advance by others about me. I had read in a magazine that the major problems the country faced were population growth and unemployment. I was an unwanted addition to both. I would greet him in the morning and apologize to him for staring at his wife's lips, hairs, and waist. I recalled that those were the only places my eyes had ever visited.

The next morning I found him cleaning the car. I gave a hesitated smile. He continued his job while ignoring me.

"Wonderful car," I commented. "Purple colored sedans are a rarity."

"Does it look like purple?" he hit back.

I was speechless. Was I going color blind? "I mean it looks like one." Oh god, what color was it!

"I need a driver. I was wondering if you know someone who is unemployed and willing to work," he said. It was confirmed, he had collected information regarding me the previous night.

"I don't know driving!" I abruptly said. It took him by surprise.

"What kind of response was that?"

"It is a fact. I am unemployed, and I don't know driving."

"If you have this attitude, then you wouldn't get a job at all."

"Yeah, nobody might give me their daughter's hand, and I would also have to die a bachelor's death!"

"You are talking something very irrelevant!" he said irritably.

"My life itself is irrelevant, exactly like this cockroach," I said and stamped my foot on a cockroach which was trying to enter his car. He looked at me in astonishment as if I were a psycho killer.

"Are you insane?" he said. He was quite shaken.

That very moment his wife arrived with the Tiffin box. She gave a dashing smile, and I smiled back. Only then did I realize the actual purpose of me interacting with him that morning. I had gone there to apologize! Instead, what a stupid thing I had done.

I kick started my bike and headed for an interview.

While I was returning from another unsuccessful interview in the evening "Sumit, Sumit," I heard a lady scream. Mrs. Avasthi was carrying two polythene bags full of vegetables and fruits. I cherished the opportunity and dropped her all the way to the home. She prepared a cup of coffee. I was seated in the drawing room.

"You know people always ask this thing to me," she said when I told her that there was so much age difference between them. "It has to be love marriage!" I emphasized.

"He wanted to get married after he had achieved something in life for which it took him 42 years. My parents were looking for a well settled guy. So that's how it happened." She was extremely talkative and lively. As per my calculations she couldn't have been more than 30.

"And you look as if you have still not attained the official age for marriage," I said. Though it was a bit too much, but was enough to evoke laughter.

"I am just out of school!" She was laughing uncontrollably. This was when Mr. Avasthi entered.

"You are not supposed to keep the door open honey," he said as he entered. Then our eyes met violently, and his face turned stony.

"Oh honey he's so funny," she said. His expression turned worse, and he gave a constipated look. I now wanted to apologize to him for my morning madness, as well. But I wouldn't do it in front of her.

"He seems to be suffering from constipation," I said on noticing his changed expression. It just came out so abruptly. Instantly I realized the blunder. She suddenly stopped laughing.

"I told na, he's so funny!" she said. He went inside the bedroom and slammed the door. I vacated the next minute. A series of unintended blunders were taking place one after the other.

Over the next few months my interaction with her, increased further. She would come to our home often and spend time with my mother. She also asked for little favors from me like getting her cell phone recharged, payment of the internet, electricity, and water bill. I also accompanied her for shopping on one occasion. Mr. Avasthi owned a local IT company and hardly found time for household chores. I was still jobless. 10 months had now passed without a job. During this time, I exchanged many cold stares with Mr. Avasthi. On several occasions, he spotted us having a jolly time together. Mr. Avasthi rarely spoke. The apologies were still due, and the numbers were only increasing. Mrs. Avasthi was my new best friend. She carried herself in a certain dignified way and always maintained the necessary distance. Harry Potter series was her favorite. She would say that Mr. Avasthi was like Ronald Weasley, she Hermione, and I were like Harry Potter in their life.

One day my father summoned me and issued a deadline. I was given one month's time to search for a job. In case I was unsuccessful then I had to forget about the job and prepare for higher studies, it was a matter of pride and proving everyone wrong now. My friends asked me to focus on my communication skills. I had been receiving an interview call from MICROMANSOFT solutions, a local company almost every week. But I had totally ignored it.

My tryst with MNCs yielded little success. My desperation grew every passing day. On the penultimate day of the month, I again got a call from MICROMANSOFT solutions. I had to go for it this time. I cleared the first two rounds of written tests along with the technical interview round. Three people were selected for the final HR round. It was a small company with 25 employees. I was mentally prepared to handle whatever came my way.

The unmistakable bloody eyes greeted me inside.

"Have your seat," he said. I knew the prospect of getting selected looked rather bleak with Mr. Avasthi at the helm, but I wanted a job badly.

"I know what is going through your mind right now. Kindly have your seat," he repeated.

I occupied the chair.

"You might be weighing your chances of selection, right?" he said coldly.

I shook my head in agreement.

"Well, let me tell you a story. Long back I had received your bio-data when I was the manager of recruitment and HR of a MNC. Three of the guys from your college were selected. But you couldn't make it. They had lesser aggregate percentage and performed poorer than you in written and technical interview rounds, still they made it. Why? They had an influential person in the company as godfather. It made things easier. Such things do happen sometimes," he paused for a moment and continued, "I revolted against the injustice and the very next day I was terminated. Then I started my own firm MICROMANSOFT solutions. The moment I saw you at the party I knew I had seen you somewhere but was unable to recall, so was staring at you. I checked your profile and your scanned photo in my email. Then I realized that you were the same guy to whom injustice was meted out. It was only coincidence that we came to stay as your neighbors."

"You are truly a man of character," I said.

"I knew that you were a deserving candidate, and you deserved a fair chance."

"You are a reincarnation of Dobby for me," I said in my enthusiasm, "I know I deserve to be selected in every interview that I attend." Then I regretted my statement.

"What is Dobby?"

"It's a weird looking house elf which saves Harry Potter's life in the famous series."

He gave the same constipated look and continued.

"I have mailed you many interview calls since then, but you never responded. In spite of being our neighbor and knowing that I owned an IT firm, never once did you bother to inquire about the company. I wondered whether you genuinely wanted a job, or it was just pretense."

"Micromansoft sounds like an undergarment brand. My friends and relatives would have thought that I had joined an undergarment store. So I ignored it completely," I said casually, and the look on his face was that of a surprise and shock. Why do I utter something silly and then repent? Why does it always happen? This was turning out to be the worst HR round of my career.

"You want this job or not?" he directly asked.

"Yes sir, I desperately want it!"

"You need to work on your communication skills a lot!"

"If I interact with you every day, I am sure my skills will definitely improve."

"Don't expect that I will sit with you and chit chat every day in case you are hired."

"Yeah, I have to work hard to earn my bread and butter," I said.

"Yeah only that can save you!" he said, "You know something, you were recommended by my wife for this job. But I don't care for any damn recommendation, what matters is the ability."

"Well thank you so much. I will serve the company to the best of my ability," I said as if he had already selected me.

"You have the ability, but your chances of getting selected are 50-50. This round has turned out to be a blunder."

"You ask me to do anything now, I will do it. You give me a last chance and see," I said brewing with confidence.

"What do you mean? This is not MTV roadies auditions that I will ask you to sing or dance and entertain me. Which last chance are you talking of? This is an HR interview round for an IT company," he said. I remained silent.

"You may leave now. You would be informed via email in case you are selected," he said.

"You can tell Mrs. Avasthi in the night, instead of sending me an email. I will get the news from her in the morning," I said.

"We follow a certain procedure. So you may leave now," he said in a serious tone. It was the same company which I had ignored for the past few months, and now I wanted a job so badly in that very company. The deadline set by father was going to end in the next 24 hours. I would be left with no other choice but to go for higher studies then, which I hated. I would be termed a failure. With the way the HR round had gone my chances of getting selected were next to impossible.

I spent a sleepless night. Early next morning I stepped downstairs, and found Mr. Avasthi cleaning his car.

"This is a purple color indeed!" I asserted.

"Yes it is," he said, "I was just checking your confidence that day."

"Yeah I always knew that. I hate purple," I said, "I couldn't have gone wrong."

He gave a deadly stare. If only I could lock my tongue using his car key, I thought. I felt as if I had nailed the last nail on my career's coffin.

"Mom has prepared a special sweet for you. I just gave it to Mrs. Avasthi."

He remained silent.

"So am I selected?"

"You will be intimated via email."

"I must learn to control my tongue."

"You need to control a lot of things," he said starting his car and speeding away. His last sentence made perfect sense.

When I knocked on their door that morning Mrs. Avasthi had opened it. I handed her the box full of sweets.

"I heard that you had a very forgettable last round?" she said.

"Yeah, I wanted to impress him but was unsuccessful. I would have rather preferred driving his car than going for higher studies."

"I know you would get this, drivers, job with or without my recommendation," Mrs. Avasthi said with a giggle.

"Am I selected for the IT job?"

"Not yet officially. Generally he wouldn't have selected if it were someone else. He hasn't discussed anything, but I read his mind."

"What's so special about me? What makes you so confident?"

"Hmmm, I am confident that he wouldn't let you flirt with me anymore."

"I didn't get you."

She smiled.

"But I never flirted with you," I asserted.

"That's what you believe. He only thinks otherwise. Now be ready to flirt with your job 24/7."

THE END

LIFE'S
SECOND OPTION

Kunal was a handsome, dynamic and a young software professional. He was hired by GK software solutions soon after his engineering. He always aspired to do something big and different. He was appointed manager of the software development team in a span of 3 years, owing to his extraordinary skills and his impressive record. He had grown closer to his boss, Saketh Roy, the CEO of the company. Career was his top priority. Saketh was his mentor and a god's gift to realize his dream. First three years had even earned him the best employee tag. Several girls at the work place, & his locality were after him; his dynamic looks impressed them the most. He stayed in a single bedroom apartment away from his conservative parents in a posh locality of Bangalore.

At the start of the fourth year, things started to change gradually. He found it difficult to concentrate on the work. His creative instincts were not at its best, and this reflected in his productivity at work. He was confused about his priorities now. Something had gone wrong, terribly wrong. The clarity with which he took decisions seemed to blur. His heart was now making decisions rather than his mind. Her attractive face, naughty smile, amazing figure, level of understanding, and cool attitude had turned him into her slave. He preferred to spend more time with her rather than at the office. His friends had predicted that it would happen. But he brushed it aside like a silly joke. His boss had great expectations from him. He enjoyed the boss's total support & didn't want to miss it at any cost. But then he didn't want to lose her either. He blamed his lack of concentration on his family and cooked up a story of ailing parents, which convinced the boss. Saketh sympathized with him and was more supportive than ever.

Kunal balanced his love & the job quite successfully, and a year passed by without any problems. His 4 year association with the company was more fruitful than his expectation. His calculations went wrong when she expressed the desire to marry him.

"Enough of hide and seek!" she said.

He was not ready for it. He was more than happy with the current arrangement. Why marry when you are happy without marriage? He couldn't put his career in jeopardy because of her, but he didn't want to lose her either. Several rounds of discussions and efforts to convince her had failed. Marriage was not an option, he tried to explain her. Marriage was the only option, she believed. Finally, a settlement was reached. They decided to flee, far away.

He knew nobody would approve of their decision. The planning and arrangement took a month's time, and the D day arrived. He would not report to duty that day. He received a number of calls from his boss, but he wouldn't pick anybody's except hers. This was something he couldn't even confide in Saketh, his mentor and confidant. How would Saketh react? When he realized that his loving wife had planned to flee with his most trusted aide!

Saketh Roy, at 35, was the most successful guy of his village. His only motive was to earn money. Money mattered to him more than success. Having come from a poor family background, he had successfully married off his five sisters in respectable families and earned a good reputation in the village. He bought a bungalow in Bangalore and a luxurious sedan in no time. The news spread like wild fire. The village Sarpanch married off his only daughter to him. Saketh was mesmerized by her beauty and was proud of having such a beautiful wife as he was just average looking with ordinarily built body and was a dwarf by society's standards. He remained busy for the most part of the day and reached home usually after 11 every night. Great responsibilities like that of a CEO come with greater challenges. An enormous time is consumed in overcoming those challenges; he tried to convey his wife. Even on weekends he had truly little time for her. Hard work was his best friend. It was the key to earning money, more and more money.

Saketh tried to please his wife by giving gifts, making her financially secure by depositing money in banks, purchasing shares, and bonds in her name.

She could have anything she wanted, except his time. He was investing the time for the betterment of their future. There was no reason for her to complain, he believed. 'Freedom enhances creativity. Creativity leads to productivity. Productivity, in turn, opens the gates to earning money. Money leads to happiness,' was what he always believed. He had given the full freedom to his colleagues (in terms of implementing their thoughts), and the company had made profits in millions. He had identified an immature, naive, but an ambitious Kunal and honed his skills. It had done wonders to the young man's confidence. Kunal was exactly like him. Hard working, dedicated, and interested in making money. Saketh gelled well with him and even gave him a free run in his personal life. Money is far more addictive than women, he believed.

Kunal would escort Kanchan, Saketh's wife, for shopping & managed all her household chores. He was available in her service when need be, and this reduced Saketh's headache. Saketh concentrated on work without worrying about her. He increased the salary of Kunal at the same time reducing his work hours. She also cherished his presence. She liked the freedom she enjoyed in Kunal's company. Even Saketh gave her freedom, but the problem was he gave her only freedom and never his company. The newly found freedom made her happy.

Sometimes unwarranted fears troubled Saketh. What if his wife fell in love with Kunal? What if the two most trusted people in his life ever betrayed him? Then his own mind provided him soothing, but highly unreliable answers. Kanchan was 7 years older than Kunal. She had Sid to take care of. Kunal being such a handsome guy definitely would have a girl friend, which Saketh wasn't sure of. In his quest for more money was he jeopardizing his personal life? He ignored the hypothetical projection and concentrated on work. Had Kunal lost focus at work? The pending project updates, his irregularity at the everyday scrum meetings, and his request to grant permission to work from home 3 days a week bore testimony to the fact that he remained more and more aloof from work. But then Kunal's parents were ailing. Saketh had to meet them to clarify and inquire about their health. There was something unusual about Kanchan's behavior also. She maintained a certain distance from him and interacted very little in whatever little time that he could spare for her. He would find out the reason soon, very soon.

Kunal and Kanchan emptied her bank vaults on the day before their scheduled flight for Delhi. She had withdrawn all her cash and turned it into gold. She wouldn't leave a clue about their whereabouts by accessing her ATM from Delhi. They tried their best to gather as much as they could think, for the security of their uncertain future. Kunal made sure that they reached home well within Saketh's arrival. She looked beautiful, yet there was fear and anxiety in those eyes. At the same time, he saw a glimmer of hope in them. Saketh's free run and her personal car, her husband's gift had helped them a lot in their preparations for a new life. They reached her home late that night. He parked the car in the spacious porch and they kissed each other passionately. They had hugged for some time before she unlocked her home's main door. It would be the longest night of her life. Little Sid greeted her at the entrance room, fully awake. On any given day, he would be fast asleep, alone. She instructed him to sleep and headed straight to the bedroom. Little Sid stared at the verandah from the window. There was darkness in the room, but the moonlit night made things clearly visible outside. Kunal had made a hurried exit moments before Saketh arrived.

Kanchan faked a headache and pretended to sleep. Saketh had to wait for his answers. His distressed soul wasn't soothed by sleep that night. He pretended to work on the laptop. She cursed his workaholic nature. He hadn't made an attempt to apply even a pain balm on her forehead. It was her last night with him after all. She wasn't sure how and where she would spend the next night and the following ones.

Early in the morning he inquired about her headache.

"It is less," she said.

"Even I have a slight headache," he said. Lack of sleep had had its effects.

She ignored his comment and readied Sid for the school. Why should she show fake sympathy? He only had a headache and not a brain tumor, she thought. The flat road had become curvy and bumpy as Saketh drove towards office. He was driving her car that morning. Sid was about to dial a number from his mother's mobile.

"Shut up and get ready for school!" she scolded and snatched the cell phone. The boy had attempted to dial Saketh's number. Under no circumstance was she going to receive his call or call him that day.

The brakes didn't seem to apply properly. He had to apply enormous power to reduce the speed. He narrowly missed hitting vehicles on the road and jumped the signal once. He also dozed off and luckily avoided being hit by a speeding truck from behind. An hour later, he considered himself lucky to have reached the office safely. He expected Kunal at that morning's review meeting, considering that Kunal had taken a leave the previous day. There was some critical task to be completed that day. But he was missing.

Only after Sid boarded his school bus, did she realize how harshly she had treated him that morning.

"Ensure he makes it to the office for the meeting," Saketh ordered his subordinate. The subordinate tried calling Kunal but in vain. The meeting began and ended without any conclusion. Saketh's temper rose like a jet plane. Kunal had not taken any prior permission nor did he call and inform anything. Saketh rang Kunal several times but in vain. He wouldn't attend calls that morning. No employee had any clue about Kunal's uninformed absentia. If there had been an emergency, Kanchan would have definitely known, Saketh thought. Kunal definitely would have kept her informed. Saketh hoped for the well being of Kunal's parents. Repeated calls to Kanchan did go unanswered. When he left the home, her phone was very much with her. With each missed call, his heart beat increased. He was never worried about her so much. Was it accidental or intentional that they both weren't receiving the call that morning? He had to find out.

In a flash, he was on his way back home continuously calling both Kanchan and Kunal, with little success. The early morning traffic delayed one hour further. The insecurity in him knew no bounds. He was never so impatient in his life before. He had to reach fast and so he took a short cut, and entered a narrow lane from the wrong side; it turned out to be one way, he was caught by the police waiting at the corner. They penalized him and made him wait unnecessarily even though he paid the money. For the first time in his life money didn't matter. In his quest for more and more money, he had made a mess of his life. He felt desperate to reach out to her. He drove faster. His mind occupied with several unreasonable and hypothetical thoughts. He accelerated at a never before speed & in spite of a sleepless night, he felt he was fully awake. The racing wheels couldn't be controlled on time. He found it harder to apply the brakes. The speeding car rammed into a waiting truck at the traffic signal. Blood trickled down his head as it rested on the steering. The mangled bumper and the crushed bonnet indicated the impact of the accident. In no time, a huge crowd had gathered.

Kanchan filled the airbag with only the basic things she would need, to start her new life. She had begun the preparations a month ago. There was still three hours before they met at the airport as promised. Her husband had made a number of calls since he left for office that morning. He had mistakenly or maybe purposely driven her car that day. She feared if he had sensed what they were up to. The fact that her insensitive husband was giving so many calls looked strange and scary. But she just didn't have the inclination to listen to his words anymore. She was fed up. Her father had ignored all her pleas and protests when he decided to marry her off to Saketh. In spite of this, she adjusted with him and played the role of a perfect housewife. She always tried to reach out to him and did her best to keep him happy. In return, she expected him to love her, spend time with her, understand & comfort her in moments of sadness and happiness. But he had failed miserably as a husband. She never expected a hard working donkey as husband. She felt isolated and unwanted. This was when Kunal entered her life. He was more a well wisher, and less a friend. This friendship had soon turned into love and then she started imagining him as her husband. But he entered her life, extremely late. God had played a dirty trick. Divorce was an option, but Saketh would not leave her so easily. He had money and power. How would her family and the society react to it? Kunal was after all much younger. The everyday role play irritated her and made her feel guilty. She couldn't stay with her husband anymore. Fleeing was the only option, painful yet best.

The most painful part was to depart from Sid. What wrong did her kid do to undergo such a severe punishment? She couldn't take him along. She didn't know her destination. She was unsure of her future. She couldn't jeopardize her son's future for her sake. It was best to leave the child with the father and let him carve out his own destiny. It would hurt, but time healed the deadliest of wounds. Right now she couldn't risk taking her son along and hoped that would be possible someday. She longed to meet him one last time and drove towards Sid's school. Driving Saketh's car made her uncomfortable. It took time for her to adjust to his sedan.

Sid stood at a distance. She raised her arms for an embrace. He stood like a statue. She hugged him; he tried to set himself free. She kissed him all over his face.

He wiped those spots in anger where she had kissed. Tears flowed from Kanchan's eyes almost instantly & uncontrollably. She was hopeful of meeting him again very soon but somewhere deep inside she feared if this were her last. He relied on her for everything. "What's wrong momma?" the little boy kept repeating, but she remained tight lipped. What would she tell him? That his momma was going away from him forever? She had a world's information to give him, instructions that would help him in life. A long list of do's and don'ts for which she had no time, she left with a heavy heart.

Kunal was already at the airport, waiting to execute plan B in the case Plan A failed. Their flight for Delhi would arrive in a couple of hours. He waited for his lady love's arrival. She had messaged him en route to the airport. He believed it was so foolish of her to have visited the school. What if somebody had seen her sobbing? What if the child suspected something fishy? What if she had changed her mind after meeting the child? He had tried so hard to keep the entire fleeing affair a secret. Every second passed nervously. He wondered if she would make it on time. Would she ever make it? He was confident that he had done the work to perfection. Yet he was nervous.

"Saketh met with an accident! Admitted in a critical condition at the Vishwa multi speciality hospital," it was an SMS sent by one of his colleagues. Was it a ploy to trace him? But he could not be fooled so easily. He dialed the directory service and extracted Vishwa hospital's number. The inquiry at the hospital revealed that Saketh was indeed admitted in a critical condition. He was suddenly in two minds.

The plan B was to stay at one of his close friend's home in Delhi and then search for a new job. Destiny would decide their fate. The life in Delhi was never easy. He would have to live under the constant fear of being tracked by the police, once Saketh registered a complaint. But the situation had suddenly changed. He had to return. Luckily if Saketh died, there would be nothing to worry. All his property would go to Kanchan. They can then marry happily. It would be the shortest route to success. But all this was possible only if Saketh died. Based on the reports that he received regarding his former boss, there was a remarkably strong possibility of that happening.

He called up Kanchan and informed her about the change in the plan. She couldn't control her emotions on hearing the news. The news of Saketh being in a critical condition brought tears in her eyes. Who would take care of Sid now? She took a u-turn just minutes away from the airport, again going back to the school to take along Sid.

The colleagues and the neighbors who received the news had already gathered at the hospital. The lounge was full of people who had come to console his family and pray for his speedy recovery. Except one person who reached a little later. Her expression impressed how disturbed she was. She definitely wanted him to be alive, even though she had decided to quit his life. Kanchan was indeed a magnificent actress, Kunal thought.

"Make sure that you don't overreact. Just pray that his soul rests in peace, and in turn lets us live peacefully," he said shockingly in her ears after having excused her away from the crowd. She remained stunned and speechless having least expected Kunal to say such a thing. She had a valid reason for disliking Saketh, yet she never wished for his death. But Kunal's career began because of Saketh. Saketh had supported him in every possible way. He was a mentor and godfather to him, yet Kunal prayed for his death? The veil of love for Kunal just seemed to lift for her that very moment, and was replaced with hatred. Kunal was a fabulous lover, but he wasn't a good human being. Anyone who wished ill for others couldn't be a good person. The next thought troubled her more. What was the guarantee that he wouldn't wish the same for her son one day? The future suddenly appeared bleak and more uncertain.

Saketh had no ill feelings for anyone and always was ready to help people. His past actions proved that he wasn't selfish. She felt angry at herself. The feeling of guilt consumed her. Seated on a bench outside the operation theatre, she prayed for her husband's well being & speedy recovery. After ten hours of emergency surgery, the doctor appeared.

"The injury to his brain is grave. We fear a partial loss of memory. He would also remain paralyzed for the rest of his life," the doctor declared. The only second chance that she expected from life had been dashed with those words.

"Isn't there any chance of him recovering fully?"

"It seems magical but is possible. Hope is the elixir of life. You have a far greater responsibility now," he said. It meant that she had no chance of leaving him now. At least she wouldn't on humanitarian grounds. A scared Sid looked at her with hope.

"God seems to have responded to only a half of your prayers. But a half dead husband comes with added benefits," Kunal whispered in her ears once the doctor had gone. He was jubilant now that Saketh was paralyzed. Kunal needn't leave the job or city, and they could continue the romance right below his nose. He had imagined a lot already. The very next moment his cheeks received the harshest treatment in years, the kind of treatment meted out to them by his father during childhood. The slap resonated in the corridor of the waiting area. She needn't explain anything. After a few minutes silence, a shocked Kunal made a hurried exit without creating a scene.

"You knew about the accident when you visited me the first time? I've never seen you cry like that before," said the ten year old Sid.

"You are maturing my son," she hugged him with tears in eyes.

"Momma, a partial memory loss, means daddy won't remember about office anymore?" he said innocently. She nodded. Sid was the only ray of hope in her life now.

"I know why you slapped Kunal uncle."

"Why?" asked a puzzled Kanchan.

"He failed the brakes of the car Nah?"

"What?"

"In the moon light, I saw him tampering with the brake in the leg space of your car. He had also opened the bonnet for some time and checked the electric cables," he said. Kunal always carried the second key of her car. This revelation was more shocking than knowing his death wish for Saketh. He was always against marriage. He liked the current arrangement.

FOURTEEN
YEARS AGO

Sankranti was nearing, and my cousin called me to plan something special for the festival. Sankranti marks the beginning of the uttarayana which is considered a conducive period for spiritual seekers. We weren't into spirituality though. It's a big festival in India.

"Let's celebrate it differently this time!" he said over the phone. I was elated to hear that.

"Do you know where we get kites in Bangalore?" he asked. I thought for a moment. I had rarely seen anyone flying kites in Bangalore in the past seven years of my stay there. I wasn't aware of any shop that sold kites or material related to it.

"Just browse the internet and you might find something," I suggested him. He agreed, and the call was disconnected after discussing general things for few minutes.

I recalled how the other day my friend had called me in the evening, asking me to find out the Ganesha temple timings on the internet. He was in need of an urgent appointment with that specific Ganesha in Basavanagudi. We are leading an e-life these days, I believe. Anything can be easily accessed by subscribing an internet connection at home.

I still remember my first tryst with computers. During seventh standard, our computer teacher asked us to be present on a particular Sunday, for special computer practical classes. Till then we had only studied about computers in textbooks. I was afraid of his strict & commanding nature. A special class was a first of its kind experience (I never attended even the weekdays classes regularly). On arriving, he called out each one of us by our register numbers, inside the computer lab. I felt like a grown up. I had heard so many fascinating things about computers. I hailed from Bidar; the whole city had only 2 major computer training institutes then. My school was one of the few esteemed institutions which boosted of a computer lab in Bidar. The only thing seniors had told me was that a computer was meant for grown-ups. One student entered the lab at a time, and the remaining was made to stand outside the class. There was only one computer inside the asbestos roofed room. The first guy came out exactly after 5 minutes and then the next guy followed. I was curious to know what was going on inside the room (what if he was conducting special viva sessions?). Before I could do something about it, the other guy came out. This guy came out 10 minutes later. Both the guys were tight lipped and looked rather excited. Finally, it was my turn.

"Sit here," the teacher said pointing towards the chair. Scared to speak anything, I did as directed.

"You know the rules?" he asked me arrogantly. I shook my head sideways indicating a no.

"Left arrow is to move the tanker to the left, right arrow for moving it right. Press the arrow pointing upwards to shoot! You have three lifelines!" His commanding tone scared the hell out of me. He wasn't conducting any viva sessions. On the pretext of taking a special class, he made everyone play a 'shoot the enemy' tanker game where the enemy tanker drops a bomb from the top. The player needs to counter them by moving his tanker accordingly and firing on the enemy tankers. If three bombs hit your tanker, then you lose that tanker. Each student was permitted to play one game. I was so scared that the first three shells fell exactly on the middle of my tanker. Same thing repeated and I lost the game in 2 minutes without dismantling any enemy tankers.

"Very poor, work on your focus and hand eye co-ordination. I expect you to shoot at least ten enemy tankers next time," he said in a disappointing tone, "Go and send the following register number inside."

I believed I was the luckiest boy in class on being sent out so soon. I vowed never to attend his special classes again. Computer games don't interest me even today. The actual challenge rests in defeating a real enemy & not virtual. The challenging games like kite flying can never be substituted by a machine game.

My cousin failed to find the web link to any shop which sold kites in Bangalore. We then headed towards the shopping area. After one hour's search, we found one in Jayanagara complex. Diamond shaped, and minis were the two varieties of kites available. We selected a 10 inch purple colored kite. A plastic spool and a roll of high quality manja were also bought. It was stupid of me to have believed that poor kite sellers would have a website of their own. They didn't even have proper sign boards in front of their shops. Moreover, kites are sold only during festivals. The very thought that I was going to be a part of a kite flying team, after 14 long years, excited and disturbed me at the same time. It brought some sweet and sour memories afresh. As if it were only yesterday that I vowed not to fly a kite, again in my life. I was twelve years old then.

14 years ago:

Dasara is celebrated joyously in my native city. The festival, which marks the victory of lord Ram over Ravana, grips the mood of the entire city. Flying kites is a major event during the festival. I was an expert in flying kites, my friends believed. I also used to prepare them from scratch. The guys in the locality appreciated the precision with which the string was tied to the smaller horizontal stick of the kite, by making tiny holes at the appropriate points. A long paper tail was also attached, for greater buoyancy and balance, to the lower end and ends of the horizontal stick. Improper tying of the string doesn't guarantee a perfect flight. It is similar to installing complicated software. You give one wrong path, and the application fails to install. But to operate it electricity is a must. The wind is always a crucial factor during kite flying. It was always available in the desired direction and in optimum levels, thus taking the kites to greater heights. Though I was always proud of my kites flying high in the sky, I doubted if that would be possible without the necessary support from one of the five vital elements of life.

I helped many of my friends except Jaggu in preparing their kites. In his case, I was a kite runner. Even though, hundreds of kites marred the evening skies, my focus was always on his kite. Jaggu was my classmate Neetu's elder brother. On one, occasion, I used special manja with an extra glassy protection, and my kite got entangled into Jaggu's ordinary quality string. The result was that his kite, which was flying high sometime ago in the blue skies, flew off & vanished in seconds. It never came back again. As they were our immediate neighbors, we had a clear view of each other. We could also directly interact with each other. Their roof had neither side walls nor railings for protection. It looked like an open ground with no boundaries. The courageous Jaggu always defied his parents' orders to stay away from the rooftop. I wore gloves for protection.

"We will teach Rishi a lesson today!" said Jaggu from his roof top.

"Sure brother!" Neetu said, loud enough to be heard by me. But she was smiling. Her petite structure, curly hairs, lively eyes, which spoke more than her words, and the beaming smile radiated an unforgettable sensation around, anybody in that sphere couldn't help ignore her.

She returned after a few minutes carrying a roll of manja which was yellow in color. Meanwhile, Jaggu challenged me for the next contest.

"This is a deadly manja bought from the patangi galli," Jaggu said proudly. Patangi galli was an area in the city where best quality manja was available. I was using a homemade manja which was bought specially from Ibad bhai. He was an expert in preparing manja and was our milkman since years. He had assured me that the manja was so sharp that it had the capability to inflict deep and painful wounds to one's skin if not handled carefully. It would have definitely taken months to cure. "This deadly manja has no competitor in the market. Use gloves for protection!" he had cautioned.

My kite was flying high proudly having won the first battle. The red diamond shaped kite looked like the star of the sky. There were several other kites, but none soared so high as mine.

Jaggu had replaced his earlier string with the new manja and beamed with excitement. With wind and Neetu's support, he managed to provide the initial flight to his black kite. It soared higher than before.

"Tread the secure path. Don't cross ways!" I warned him.

"Brother let's do as he says and enjoy kite flying," said Neetu.

"I knew you were scared," he said to me, ignoring Neetu's request.

"It was my duty to warn you. History will surely repeat itself," I said.

He tried to entangle his string into mine. I thoughtfully prevented it by directing my special manja slightly away. It also ensured that his kite was safe, and Neetu could spend more time on the roof helping and cheering him.

"Let's not get into a kite war again. You have lost one already!" I reminded him.

"Yes brother he's right. Let me enjoy the kite flying," she said.

"On whose side are you?" he questioned irritably.

"Of course yours," she said forcibly. I knew she was always on my side. She shared secret information about the quality of his manja. She shared her private notes and helped me in my homework, much against Jaggu's wish.

"I've got him this time," he shouted. His manja had entangled into mine. I let loose the roll. My kite flew higher owing to the added length to the existing manja. He looked puzzled. In a bid to save his kite, he had reached the edge of the roof. The moment my manja slashed his, he lost balance and fell from the roof. His kite flew away never to be back again. Neetu screamed in horror as she saw her only brother fall. She was in a state of shock. I jumped my roof to land on theirs. I quickly went towards the end from where he had a nasty fall. Their house was single storied.

"Thank god he fell in the bushes," I said. She looked shockingly at me. The shock on her face had then turned into a puzzled expression.

"I am not lying," I said. The next moment, she ran downstairs without responding.

We took him to a nearby hospital. The physician who attended to him termed Jaggu lucky in spite of the nasty fall. He had only fractured his right hand and leg and received 20 stitches to his head. His parents barred both of them from kite flying and a visit to the roof, instead of safeguarding it by building the railings.

I apologized to Neetu though I wished Jaggu a speedy recovery.

"It was an accident. Moreover, you shouldn't be apologizing to me," she said & confessed that she missed the kite flying experience.

"Won't you miss me?" I asked.

"Whether we fly kites or not, we still are neighbors. And we would get to see each other daily," she said with a grin. Before the next festival, their father incurred a huge financial loss in business and had sold their home. They left the city also and went into oblivion.

After that incident, I attempted several times to fly the kite, but the excitement was missing. I dearly missed them both. I emotionally wrote phrases like "Jaggu I am sorry," "Jaggu can never beat me," "Jaggu is scared," "Neetu I miss you," on my kites. Even though, my kites soared high as ever, there was no one to challenge me. I missed the ever cheerful and energetic Neetu. I was filled with her memories whenever I went on top of the roof. There was a sense of guilt and loneliness. I stopped visiting it one day and vowed never to fly kites again in my life.

January, 2009: "We could have celebrated the festival by having dinner in a resort," I said while heading back home. My cousin had planned to pick my sister-in-law and nephew from home and head towards the open ground.

"What's wrong with you? We found the kite shop and also all the necessary material to make it fly. You were also an expert in kite flying during your childhood days!" My puzzled cousin said.

"Long back I vowed never to fly kites again," I said.

"So what!"

"I can't go kite flying with you because of that."

"Stop behaving like a Bhishma Pitamaha," he said. The famous Bhishma Pitamaha of Mahabharata had vowed to remain a bachelor all through his life, and never become the king of Hastinapura.

"I am quite serious about it," I retorted.

"You can at least assist us in flying it," he said.

"Yeah I suppose I can," I agreed reluctantly.

Various college students were playing cricket in the ground when we reached. We occupied a small open area in a corner, and I readied the kite for its flight. My cousin held the kite in his hands at a distance and my 7 year old nephew held the string trying to provide the initial flight. My sis-in-law was busy taking the video shoot of our unique outing. The kite flew for a few seconds and crash landed. They attempted several times but due to the lack of wind it again met the same fate. I watched them struggle.

"Rishi can't be a mere spectator," protested my sister-in-law.

"Kaka, this kite is bad. It doesn't fly at all," said my nephew.

"Come on dude. You're vow is spoiling our outing," said my cousin.

Their frustrated and helpless faces had put me in a fix. I decided to break the vow and enter the arena. There was extremely little time to think. The glow returned on their faces. They expected a lot.

"Let's draw something on the kite & make it more attractive before we attempt to fly it again," said my sister-in-law. I didn't think it was a wise idea but agreed.

Me and my nephew started drawing on it using sketch pen. He drew an elephant. I recalled Jaggu's face and attempted to draw. But it resembled a zombie. I was careful not to tear off the plastic made kite while highlighting my drawing skills.

"Interesting drawings!" she said.

"No wind in this direction. Bad luck!" said my cousin pointing in the northern direction. I nodded in unison. I had taken the command now & was controlling the flight by holding the string. My cousin was holding the kite at a distance and all set to leave it, on sensing the wind speed.

"Let's try in the opposite direction for good luck," said my nephew. We smiled. After a few attempts, the kite met the same fate and landed several times on the ground with a thud. We took a break of five minutes.

"See the wind is blowing, hurry up & hold the string!" screamed my cousin.

Even before I could make an attempt to hold it, the wind stopped blowing. Every time we felt the change in the wind speed we tried to fly the kite. Each time it crash landed. After several failed attempts, we decided to head back home. Even though our idea of flying the kite failed; the idea of having a unique outing succeeded.

In the midst of all these, I realized that I wasn't the same magician with the kites anymore. There was an enormous difference between now and then. Like how computers aren't only used for playing games, you can even attempt to find a kite shop on it. In that hour of failure, there was still something which remained unchanged. I badly missed a cheerful Neetu.

"Looks like the wind god is angry at me for breaking the vow," I said to my cousin.

"He seems to be on a holiday too!" he said.

As we headed towards the exit, my nephew screamed innocently, "Kaka, the wind is blowing again!"

THE END

THE VALENTINE'S DAY

The readers might find this story a regular one. What's the big deal in the story? Such things do happen, some readers might say. A writer shouldn't turn every such incident into a story and publish it into a book, they might argue. I completely agree with all such apprehensive readers and endorse their views. Even I turned down the offer to include this story into my collection, but the protagonist wouldn't relent. This was the only occasion in his life when he had done some heroics. For he has done several crooked things in his life. I was arm twisted when I out rightly rejected his offer to write a story on him, let alone include it. In spite of him being my best friend.

"You, so called writers, only need a spicy thing to report," Rakesh complained.

"Yeah, people prefer only spicy, interesting things!"

"Even you can add some spice to my story and make it interesting," he said.

"Okay let's change your name to Ranbir and your girl friend's name to Deepika then. That would be the first step towards making a spicy recipe," I said.

"Idiot fellow then it wouldn't remain my story. Use my original name, Rakesh. Smitha is a much better name than Deepika," he said.

"Ok, but I take no responsibility if it turns out to be boring," I cautioned.

"If it turns out to be boring then you should stop writing," he suggested.

"Whatever it is, I would be surely including a warning for the readers at the beginning of the story. Let them read at their own risk," I said.

"Fine, in spite of that, everybody would read it," he said confidently.

The story thus begins, along with my genuine opinions in italics at the end of some paragraphs. The rest is how Rakesh wanted it to be, it might include his imagination too. It's his story, his way, narrated by me.

Smitha was a 1st year B.Com student at the prestigious RK College in Bangalore. She was beautiful, intelligent, and attractive like most girls. She had many admirers and her classmate Rakesh was one among them. She always liked helping others and sympathized with him as he was unable to clear the first year exams during the past three attempts. Nobody in the class was interested in making friendship with him, but she had no such reservations. Their friendship developed during the course of time and she considered him one of her best friends. *'Nobody' is just an exaggeration. There might have been some people, but that is unimportant for the story. Why was she attracted only towards this guy? Only god knows.*

She hated the attitude of her parents. Her father had strictly instructed her not to interact with any male in college; it included her male faculties too. Her mother kept a strict vigil; she even checked Smitha's call records and SMS. Smitha hated her mother's spying habit and had an argument with her on many occasions. But her mother wouldn't give it up so easily. It was her old habit. Smitha found it difficult to hide her everyday interactions with Rakesh from her mother. He was famous for only wrong reasons. When Smitha's family and friends first came to know that she had befriended Rakesh, they read out an entire report on him and cautioned her not to take the relation further. "We are just friends," Smitha answered. *Detective mother and an ultra strict father are found in great numbers throughout the world. Girls like freedom and they should get it without much fuss.*

"Rakesh is not the guy for you. Listen to what your father says. A guy never keeps his commitment when it comes to friendship with a girl; guys are ambitious and somehow trap the poor girls in their love," her mother had given a generalized opinion on all the boys in the world. 'Does it include her father?' Smitha thought. Her parents after all had a love marriage. *I guess the story of her parents, how her father had trapped her innocent mother into his love web, would have made for a definitely interesting read. But Rakesh wouldn't listen. Anyway let's continue with his boring story.*

"He is cunning, shrewd, & knows how to brain wash girls. He had even proposed me, but I straight away rejected him," Sonali, her close friend, had informed.

"Didi he smokes, drinks, & eats chicken," Rohan, her younger brother, reported. *I am sure; her father too did all the above three.*

"Guys like him spend their time only after girls. Tell me one field in which Rakesh excels? You have a bright future only if you keep good company. He has been failing in the exams for the past three years," the principal had advised, on her mother's insistence. *Sometimes a mother can go to any extent to save her daughter from a bad influence. I know Rakesh excelled in wooing girls.*

In spite of many such warnings and suggestions, Smitha found it difficult and unreasonable to break her friendship. She had obeyed her parents all through her school days. She excelled in studies and also showed interest in household activities as per her parents' wishes. All her teachers were proud of her. Most of her early days had already gone in making others happy. Luckily, she had found an understanding friend in Rakesh and now everyone was opposed to her! Why make such a big fuss about it? Didn't she have the right to make friends of her choice? Did she need permission even to make friends? There was a strong rumor that they were dating each other. Rakesh had advised her to ignore what others said. *Rumors are always meant to be ignored. Start taking them seriously only when it involves you.*

Rakesh had clarified to Smitha that, he never in his wildest of dreams had approached or proposed Sonali. And she believed him. Sonali lived in a dream world of her own where she had been proposed by people like Brad Pitt, Akshay Kumar, Hritik Roshan, Tom Cruise to name a few. Rakesh's proposal was bound to be rejected. *Hope Sonali finds her Tom Cruise. Why would she lie? I trust Sonali. To be frank, I find her more interesting than Smitha.*

Rohan was after all a kid. Who doesn't smoke these days? Even many popular film stars smoked openly on screen, and it was cool. Smitha somewhere read that limited intake of alcohol was always good for health. She had no figures to verify if Rakesh's intake exceeded that limit. She found no reason why his good or bad habits should affect their relationship. She was put through a test when he desperately wanted to meet her on a Valentine's Day. She believed that it was a day meant for lovers to hangout and his insistence was a bit strange. *Only one question, why select V-day for a date?*

Rakesh argued that when they were not in love, there was no harm in meeting. He wanted to take her out for lunch and nothing else. She insisted him to postpone his plan, but he wouldn't agree. After giving it a thought, she decided to join him on the V-day. Her parents had insisted her to stay indoors that day. But she had convinced them that she had to accompany her best friend, Sonali, in buying a gift for her beloved. Her lunch with Rakesh had to be a secret. Her father had even sighted that some fanatic group had decided to target young couples celebrating Valentine's Day, and it was safe if she stayed indoors. She was in no mood, to listen. *Sonali finds a lover! I am sure Smitha would be spied by her mother. The only thing she could do to avoid it would be to invite Sonali to her home and leave home along with her. Why would Sonali agree to that, when she had advised her to keep away from Rakesh? Why did he choose only that particular day? So many questions but let's not lose focus.*

Rakesh's father was a world renowned doctor. He appeared on numerous discussion panels on health related issues on News channels. He provided free treatment to the needy and was remembered by many for his good deeds. Rakesh grew up watching his father keep busy all the time. His mother spent most of her time in socializing & showed little interest in her son's studies and his childhood. He took to alcohol at a very young age. When he was in tenth, his friends took him to a dance bar. He was also involved in a drunken brawl on that occasion. Actually he wasn't drunk, one of his friends had passed a sleazy comment on his mother and that had irked him. He beat up the boy black and blue, and this was highlighted by the media. The media never pointed out what actually led to the altercation, but they just tarnished his father's name. *The episode caused much embarrassment to the father son duo. Media needs spicy things to report, and if someone provides it so easily, then why the media should not publicize it? Amitabh played a role similar to Rakesh's in 'sharabi'.*

Another infamous incident, which damaged Rakesh's reputation, was when a girl named Kavya, his mother's best friend's daughter and also his classmate, had spread a rumor that he had raped her. Rakesh confronted her after she said that. People instantly believe girls without cross verification. Later it was proved that he was innocent, and the girl had lied. *But the majority believes that the wealthy doctor had hushed up the case, and reached a settlement with the victim to protect his son and his own reputation. I believe she lied.*

Rakesh could never concentrate on studies. The everyday quarrel and blame game between his parents regarding his irresponsible upbringing took its toll on him. Girls at college hardly interacted with him, and many of his friends had already graduated. He felt lonely and depressed. This was the time when Smitha joined the college. He had never seen such a beautiful & intelligent girl in his life. When the entire world had branded him a villain, she considered him reasonable and interacted with him freely. She didn't mind what others said. He started showing interest in studies, and they spent most of their time in the library. She promised him that she would make sure he got promoted this time. He even dropped her home on a few occasions. His depression had started to wither away. *I can sense, where the story is headed. It's too predictable. Of course, Rakesh would pass this time! What else did you think?*

THE V DAY:

They met at the 'Pizza Hut' for lunch. She was curious to know the reason behind their meet on that particular day. He didn't want to hurry and asked her to be patient. They ordered a tomato soup, and a spicy pizza with cheese. The order would take some time. Smitha revealed how she had lied to her parents and made it a point to meet him. He expressed his happiness and pointed out that he knew for sure she would come. Just when the conversation began, a group of 20 odd fanatics who had pledged to target couples celebrating Valentine's Day, suddenly barged inside and gheraoed them. The soup & pizza were yet to be tabled.

"Are you brother and sister?" one of them asked.

"No!" he said.

"Don't you know, dating on Valentine's Day is a crime?" shouted another guy.

"But, we are just friends!" Smitha said.

"Everyone says the same thing when we catch them red handed," said the first guy.

"You are nobody to advice us what to do," she protested.

"Is it? This is India and not America!" said another.

"We know that you love each other, and in spite of our repeated warnings on TV, you have decided to date today. Now it's our job to take your relation to a logical conclusion," said a middle aged guy.

"What do you mean?" she asked.

"We are going to get you married!" the guy responded.

"Yes, marriage is the only solution," shouted the others in unison.

What a dramatic turn of events. They would get married, and their parents cannot even blame the two. There was also a priest in the group. Smitha shivered at their revelation. She had come there only on Rakesh's insistence, and marriage was a very remote thing as far as she was concerned. What would she tell her parents when they would question her later on? She would lose all her credibility in case those people succeeded in getting her married to Rakesh. She had never been in such a situation before in her life, and never loved Rakesh. Her eyes turned moist & face was pale.

"Please don't do that. I beg your pardon!" she pleaded before the group. She was on her knees begging for forgiveness.

"Rakesh do something. Tell them that we are not lovers!" she spoke in desperation while she wept.

The sight of Smitha pleading before him and others made him feel worse. He had to make a decision. Her moistened eyes and panicked expression melted him. He finally spoke. *I knew he would do something appreciable.*

"Nobody is going to force us into marriage. Please get up!" he said ensuring that she stood up with his support.

"Whom the hell are you to stop us?" A guy thundered.

Rakesh wasn't intimidated by their aggressive posture and put up a brave front.

"I am going to stop you people!" he said and dared them to touch either of them and be ready to face the consequences.

When a few among the crowd headed aggressively in his direction and were about to hit him, one of the guys shouted at them to stop. He identified Rakesh as the son of the famous doctor Bhandari. He told the others, how the doctor was instrumental in saving the life of his daughter. The guy seemed to be a very prominent member of the group and others paid heed to his words. They decided to retreat while cautioning them not to repeat such a mistake next time. *Why did the good Samaritan recognize Rakesh so late?*

Smitha heaved a sigh of relief and hugged Rakesh. She was in tears. Rakesh begged her forgiveness. He dropped her back home in his car. They maintained silence throughout the journey. He could have easily used the situation to his advantage and tricked her into marriage, but he didn't. It spoke volumes about his integrity and his character. He had even taken the moral responsibility for the incident. She felt comforted &

secured in his company. She was joyful. On reaching the destination, he begged her forgiveness again.

"You wanted to say something before the incident took place?" she asked.

"Nothing!" he said.

"Please tell me!" she insisted.

"Really nothing!" he repeated and bid her goodbye.

She kept waving at him as he left. Their relation had grown by leaps and bounds during the day. Love was in the air. And the air carried the message to her mother, who was watching Smitha wave continuously in the same direction, long after the car vanished from sight. *I salute your heroics my friend. Sometimes silence does unimagined wonders than words. I expected you to open your heart and reveal your feelings. I doubt whether the fanatics' entry was actually a random event. It could have been staged! But then I believe Rakesh when he says it wasn't.*

THE END

2040

It worries me when I think about the future. Whatever field we consider, the humans have taken giant strides. Be it agriculture, science and technology, fashion, communication, or astronomy to name a few. The entire world is at the finger tips these days thanks to the internet. It makes one happy to think about the positives. But when we look at the increasing pollution levels, deforestation, acts of terrorism, and rise in the number of nuclear weapons, it makes one sad. I occasionally care about the nature, or earth. I am happy with the way my life has shaped up. I have a loving and understanding family, a satisfactory job, helpful friends, and other necessary things needed for life which might be bracketed as luxury by few. Last night I pondered over the way mother earth is shaping up. What would happen if the same persists? How would be things in 2040? I let my imagination loose, and it returned with a headache. Everything changed in these three decades except few things. Let's sail together to find out.

A hot summer in 2040:

Solar energy is being used as a fuel for vehicles. The average temperature in all the major cities of India is reported at 60 degree Celsius. Petrol pumps are a thing of the past. The plastic headgear that I am wearing while driving my 'air car' has a coolant. A person can only think when he maintains his cool. The coolant has to be refilled every month at the authorized government agencies. The road is not the popular mode of transportation anymore. Heavy congestion due to the increased number of vehicles has forced several people to buy 'air cars'. It's mandatory by the government that everyone obtains a flying license. A set of regulations is enforced on birds. There are specific lanes demarcated for birds and humans. The birds have learnt discipline after years of flying freely in the sky. They know they cannot violate the boundaries; the moment they do it, a low voltage current strikes, forcing them into their allotted path. I am heading for my close friend's 25th anniversary function. I currently reside in Bengaluru (popularly known as Bangalore earlier).

"Do you want to call Anand?" my smart phone questions.

"No," I reply. It says sorry and sleeps.

A number of advanced gadgets have entered the market and are available on the internet. The delivery time is reduced to one hour for the product bought online. It's a faster world. I search for a gift that I would be presenting them. I find a memory lock meter. It's a newly launched product in the market. It senses a person's thoughts. A person just needs to wrap the meter which comes with a belt around his head, and think of some past incident in his life. A click on the gadget's lock button at that moment captures the thought and provides the photograph. The clarity of the picture depends on the person's ability to remember, and visualize things. I am sure there are certain thoughts, which my friend would want to share with his wife. If a person tries to create a false image, something which never occurred in his/her life, then the gadget detects it and issues a warning. It has super intelligent sensors. What if my friend's uncontrolled mind ventures into the secret darker portion of his memory? The gift would be then turning into a curse. It won't be appropriate. I need to present something which personifies romance so that he can share it with his beloved. What better than a red rose?

The Lalbagh is the only place left with roses. It's a highly secure area. Roses are issued on special requests and require written permission from a specific government agency. Illegal sale or purchase of rose results in a jail term of up to five years and a fine of up to 10 lakh rupees. The atmosphere conducive for the growth of the rose is artificially maintained at select places. Lalbagh is one among them, the only one in Bengaluru. I am sure Anand and Sudha would be glad to receive a bunch of roses on their 25th anniversary, or else they would have to be satisfied with artificial flower made bouquets only.

"Do you want to call the CRIAI?" my smart phone questions.

"Yeah," I respond.

"I am glad to be at your service," it answers and does its job.

I contact the 'Certified Rose Issue Authority of India (CRIAI)' over the 8g network; in our times 3g was the latest. 8g has been path breaking. You need to make some setting changes in your cell phone, and connect it to the headgear which contains the coolant using a port. The smart phone detects the thoughts, and automatically understands the user's needs and questions accordingly. It's a mobile mini robot. The gadget is the best product of human imagination so far. The phone connects and the official answers.

"I presume you are thinking of roses and Lalbagh, Mr. Kumar!" the moment the call was made, the reason was also communicated to the official via a text on his screen.

"Yeah, I would reach in 10 minutes time. Kindly register my request for four red roses."

"May I know the exact reason for which the rose is needed?"

"It will be presented as a gift."

"Kindly wait while I check your past transactions, and verify your Lalbagh membership for the renewal dates," he says and puts me on hold. The advanced Aadhar cards are linked with each person's phone number. Any information regarding the customer is available by punching his phone number. A background check is a must before further communication. Every member is only allowed up to 12 free red roses a year, owing to the increase in population. Apart from that, 12 white, 12 pink, and 12 free yellow roses are issued per person per year.

"Sorry sir, your quota of 12 red roses is already used up."

"What? This is my first request in 2040!" I complain.

"But the system shows that your quota is already full. You can still opt for a white or a yellow rose."

"It might be a system error, kindly recheck."

"The update is done for every transaction, and we have a foolproof system. There isn't a possibility of any system fault."

"Register a complaint then!"

He disconnected the call on his official number, and called back using his private number. The official calls are monitored for quality and security reasons.

"Now we can talk freely," he says.

"There is some error," I repeat.

"Yeah, I know. Some minister had consumed his quota and got himself more roses from your quota," he says.

"This is theft!" I protest.

"But nothing can be done. There are lots of cases already pending in the courts, and in spite of the advanced technology the government is finding it hard to dispose them off. You wouldn't want one more case getting added to the list!"

"What should I do?"

"Pay me 4000 rupees and I shall get you four fresh red roses without any fuss," he says.

"Am I supposed to pay bribe when my free quota is still intact?"

"The quota is full. Are we going to discuss the same thing again?"

"From where are you going to arrange the flowers for me?"

"It isn't your headache," he says reassuringly.

I arrive at Lalbagh and park my 'air car' on the ground. A huge mass of land is covered with serene plants and trees, making it the most refreshing place. The lush green stretch of land reminds me of my college days when I used to visit the place frequently with my girlfriend. The green cover can be seen from a distance. But two levels of security should be cleared to enter it. A security check is conducted at the gate where my Lalbagh life membership is verified. The Lalbagh life membership card is available with only me and Anand, among our friends. After the verification, I am allowed to the next level. I punched in my phone number and scanned my smart phone, for 2nd round of authentication. The second gate opens, and I am greeted by the same official. He escorts me inside.

The trees are preserved in patches. Highly effective and advanced chemicals known as TIC (Tree Injecting Chemicals) are being used to inject life into the trees and plants to keep them alive. The process of injecting chemicals into trees has opened up several job opportunities for the country's youth. The process has to happen every day for prolonged greenery. Potable water is at an all time low and is available scarcely at selected places during monsoon. Only in certain states of the country which had sensed the importance of trees and preserved the forests, do we find a sufficient amount of potable water. A talented team of Chinese scientists has developed a formula to produce artificial water to fight water scarcity. The water is exported to India every alternate day. Some people say artificial water tastes better than the natural water which they used to drink every day, a few years ago. I wonder how that is possible when water is colorless, tasteless, and odorless.

"Take your flowers," the official says and hands me four fresh red roses. A chit is also passed to me; it carries his Swiss bank account number. Some things don't change even after decades. I electronically transfer the money and head towards the exit.

My next destination is Anand's house. I am sure nobody would be presenting him roses. Sudha loves them, but poor Anand cannot afford to visit Bengaluru on the day of his anniversary just for them. He doesn't own an 'air car' also. He is poor by current standards. Luckily, he has a Lalbagh membership card.

"Hello Kumar, Your request for a site on Moon has been accepted and is under process," I receive a recorded message on my smart phone. It makes me happy. I would be soon joining the elite group. The real estate market on the moon has caught the imagination of the nation. 30 years ago when a foreign firm began allotting land on the moon to interested individuals with authentic registration certificates, the idea was rejected by the majority considering it insane. Now the situation is such that people need at least one site on moon badly. They know the deteriorating situation on earth; it's devoid of any bright hopes for their future generations. There is no space to walk, forget buying a piece of land. The process of transporting people on the moon has already begun. I had bribed the broker for a site with better scenic view. "The great wall of China is visible from your site. Congrats on becoming a Moonite," I receive a text message from the broker. The registration is complete.

My nose itches. It is high time, I replaced the old worn out plastic inhalers and replaced them with the latest ones. The tiny oxygen inhalers cleanse the polluted air and extract oxygen from it. They then supply the oxygen using tiny pipes connected internally. They are placed right on the nose like a nose ring. They come in different shapes and sizes. I have selected the one which resembles a honey bee.

A novice driver misses hitting me by inches. I put on the 'distance alarm' warning him to keep away. He speeds away.

After a two hours journey, I reach Gulbarga 650 km from Bengaluru. Gulbarga is popularly a dry place. A number of 'air cars' are already parked in front of Anand's house. The entrance room is decorated with a number of flowers like jasmine, daisy, lilac, tulip, orchid, and hydrangea. They are made from a distinct synthetic plastic. They even let out fantastic aroma. It's difficult to distinguish between the original and the fake ones. It was an invention by German scientists.

"Kumar has finally arrived!" declares Anand.

Sudha comes forward to welcome me. The aroma of the roses instantly catches her attention.

"Wow! Roses from Lalbagh?" she remarks. I present her the fresh red roses which have come a long way from Bengaluru. They were hidden in an air conditioned tiny metallic container which protected them from heat all through the journey.

"I was meant to present them to her," rues Anand.

"It's a present for both of you."

"Hey, where's Sumana (my wife) and the rest of your family?" asks Sudha.

"They are in Kashmir, to beat the heat."

"Pakistan has strongly sought the help of U.S. to solve the Kashmir issue this time!" says Anand.

"And India has clarified that Kashmir is an integral part of our nation!" I say with a smile.

"You people are always discussing politics, even during a function," Sudha complains. She offers me drinks and heads towards other guests. She thanks me profusely for presenting such a valuable gift. As anticipated, nobody had presented them with original red roses.

"You've finally managed to bring a smile on her face," says Anand.

"What happened?"

"She was all fired up and blasted me for being highly unromantic. She wanted something unique today."

"Then?"

"I just called up the CRIAI to order red roses, and realized that I've been duped."

"How is that?"

"Only yesterday I had checked with them, and the system showed that I could still obtain 4 free red roses from my allotted quota. I only need to pay transport charges. But when I called the official an hour ago, he said I've used all 12."

"Then what have you decided?" I ask. My roses might have been allotted from his quota.

"To purchase a bunch of roses illegally," Anand says.

"You know it's punishable under law?"

"How many are punished till now?"

We exchange smiles, and the party continues.

THE END

THE UNANSWERED QUESTION

"**H**i dear," she SMSed.

"Hi," I replied.

"R u leavng?"

"Yeah."

"At wht tme?"

"6:30 P.M. by a KSRTC bus."

"OMG, wht a tmng!"

"Wht?"

"Dad is schduld to leave at d same tme."

"Ur dad in Bnglur? By whch bus is he leavng?"

"By d KSRTC's Airawath a/c."

"I hve my seat bukd in d same bus!" I SMSed.

"Yuppy! Here's ur chnce 2 imprss hm."

"Dn't wry, I hold a master's in imprsing pple."

"I knw, u r d bst."

"Dat's y I hve d mst beautiful grl in the twn as my grl frnd."

"Thn wht els?"

"Catch u aftr sumtme. Muaaahh. Bye."

And I ended our short messaging session (SMS chat). That was my girlfriend Nisha. I am Nitin. I glanced through my portion of the room. I had packed everything. My airbag and suitcase were both ready. A day before I had shifted all heavy luggages to Bidar through the railways. The room bore a deserted look. Two of my roommates had already shifted. The hostel and especially our room were full of precious memories. I would be cherishing them forever.

The door opened with a bang.

"All set to leave?" Anuj asked. He was my roommate for four years, and my best friend.

"Yes buddy."

"How was today's exam?" he asked excitedly.

"It was easy."

He was so very excited at the prospect of completing the exams. "I am overjoyed. Our jail term in this hostel has ended finally after four years of struggle," he said. The hostel rules were strict and we fancied breaking them.

"I am undergoing mixed emotions. I will miss so many things, especially you!" I said.

"Yes I do agree with you," he said with a smile.

The ability to take quick decisions, which always proved to be correct, is what made me feel proud of myself. The moment I met Anuj for the first time, I knew that he was 'my type' of guy. It proved to be correct. We had a blast during the past four years of our life.

"Today is Ananya's b'day, isn't it?" I asked. Ananya was Anuj's girlfriend.

"Yes," he said with a smile. Her birthday was the reason he had decided not to shift on that day. She was one of our classmates and resided in Bangalore with her parents.

"I have something for her," I said taking out a nicely packed and decorated tiny box from my suitcase.

"A gift! She's my girlfriend!" He said with a smile.

"Give it to her on her brother's behalf," I said ignoring his comment, "It has the watch, the one which she liked the most the other day. You remember?"

"You mean the sleek Titan one? It runs into thousands."

"Does it matter in friendship?" I shot back. Presenting costly gifts was a trend.

"Why don't you stay today? We will party hard."

"Sorry dude, but I don't want to miss the opportunity to impress my soon-to-be father-in-law," I said while mentally chalking out the plan. "You leave now, it's already 5:00 P.M.," he said smartly. I placed the airbag across my right shoulder and held the suitcase in the other hand. Anuj insisted on carrying my suitcase till the hostel gate and bid an emotional adieu. We promised each other to keep in touch always.

I hired an auto and headed towards Bangalore bus-stand. It was 5:30 P.M. already.

"I have a bus at 6:30. Kindly drive faster," I told the driver.

"Don't worry. We will be there in 20 minutes," he said as if he were a formula one champion. The time passed quite fast.

"It's already 6:00 P.M. and you have not even covered half the distance," I complained. He was driving extremely slowly adding to my desperation.

"Hello Mister, can't you see the traffic jam?" he shot back angrily. "Do you want me to crash into some vehicle?" I wanted to suggest that it was a matter of pride for him, and his auto, that a genius like me, was traveling in it.

Then we were struck at the junction, the signal had stopped working. The traffic inspector had a tough time managing it. I had little hopes of the jam clearing up on time. I took out the photo of my dearest Nisha from the wallet. Blue mysterious eyes, fair and smooth skin, slim figure, petal like soft lips, and slightly blonde hair, she looked like a Barbie.

The cell phone started ringing. It was Nisha's call.

"Hi dear," I spoke.

"Hi," she said in a worried tone. This, in turn, worried me.

"What happened?"

"Someone stole dad's luggage, wallet, and mobile phone from the hotel room. He had just called from a telephone booth." Her father Mr. Murlidhar owned a chain of hotels in Bidar. He paid frequent visits to Bangalore. She continued, "Everyone at home is worried." I could have only sympathized with her as I was in a sympathetic situation struck in the middle of a jam with high probability of reaching late and losing the bus.

"Are you there?" she queried.

"Yeah, let's hope that the thief is soon caught. And your dad gets the valuables back."

"That's ok, but I am more worried about something else."

"What is it?"

"He might have lost the ticket, and he might miss the bus tonight. Your real chance of impressing him is then gone."

The buses to Bidar ran jam packed & the possibility of finding another bus so quickly was remote. I wondered if I would also miss the bus. The traffic showed no signs of easing out. Luckily, after five minutes the traffic started moving slowly. What if he really missed the bus! I didn't want that to happen.

"Let's hope that he hasn't lost the ticket. In case I find him in the bus, I will let you know. Don't worry," I said.

"You are a big idiot. Have you seen my daddy ever? How are you going to recognize him?" I had met her several times but never seen her father, even though he was a famous personality in the city of Bidar.

"The most handsome man in the bus would be your dad. It's as simple as that," I said, in my bid, to impress her.

"Oh, why is that so?" she asked naughtily. The daddy centric chat was slowly shifting momentum.

Looking at the driver's face I responded, "A fairy's dad would never look like a devil."

"Do I look like a fairy?" she sweetly asked.

Even though I had explained the resemblance between her and fairy several times, she never lost an opportunity to ask it again. I hated this habit of hers, but I loved her the most.

I started, "In case fairies exist then there is no doubt that you are one of them. The moments we spent together have been nothing less than a heavenly experience. You make me feel as if I am the prince of fairy land. If I take a snap of your lips and rose petals together, people would get confused which is what? The soft skin of yours is a testimony to the fact that god's finish is smoothest than any other finishing touch in the world."

"Your fantasy stories are something which turn me on and make me fall in love with you again," she said.

"Your blonde hairs are silkier than silk. Government should appoint a commission to probe your hair's silky character," I continued.

She laughed her heart out.

"So sweet of you sweetest sweetu," I said.

"Tell me what's special today?" she asked.

"Your dad has lost his valuables, and I am about to lose the bus," I said. This joke didn't go down well with her.

"I asked you seriously. It's about us!" she said.

"It's 15th of June and 3 years ago I had proposed you on the very same day. Many of my friends said that I shouldn't hurry, but that's how I am, always quick and correct." She was impressed by my memory and kissed me via phone. I kissed her back with a noticeable amount of sound.

"Brother, if you are done with kissing then you may get down. We've reached," said the driver. I bid her bye and handed the auto driver 100 rupees while thanking him for reaching on time.

Most of the seats in the bus were already occupied. Only a few minutes remained for the departure. My seat number was 25, at the back. I placed my luggage in the luggage space above the seat. It was now time to execute my plans.

I showed the bus conductor my ticket, at the same time checked the reservation list, to ensure the number of seats reserved. Mr. Murlidhar's name was found against number 26. The window seat next to me was no.26. My decision to reserve seat no. 25 was perfect. I felt proud and congratulated myself for having made the right decision again. There couldn't have been a bigger coincidence than us having reserved our seats next to each other. Even god was playing a positive role in my love story. In a few minutes, the bus started. The seat next to me was vacant. Had Mr. Murlidhar lost his ticket then he would be unable to board the bus. Sending tickets via SMS weren't a trend those days. Would he be boarding it from some other stop? I hated this confusion. I didn't want to miss the golden opportunity.

The next moment there was a text message from Nisha. It was a forwarded message, "The three harmful things in the world are :-> Love, selfishness, and over confidence, the three most beautiful things in the world are-> girls, hope, and confidence. So let's make our life the most beautiful."

"I dn't agree with u at al. Hw cn luv be hrmful? Bcoz of luv my lif is beautiful. I am cnfidnt tht I wud definitely imprs ur father one day and marry you," I replied via SMS.

The bus came to a halt near a pick up spot in the outskirts of the city.

A man in his fifties boarded the bus and sat next to me. He was whitish with slightly brownish hair indicating that he dyed them regularly. He wore a white shirt untugged over a dark blue pant. His wrist watch was missing. He wore a grim look and was carrying a suitcase. I greeted him with a smile, but he ignored.

I messaged Nisha and asked her to describe her father.

"A hrd wrkr, a patient listner, wid a heart of gold, and d brain of a genius, his laugh is awesum and freaky. He turns a philosopher suddnly and d nxt momnt he cracks d mst cmplicatd joke. He's d bst daddy," she replied. She had a habit of saying irrelevant things whenever I expected sanity from her, and this happened frequently.

"Did your dad call you again?" I sent another message without using any short cuts.

"No."

"Explain his looks."

I was addicted to SMSing, so I decided against calling her. I wouldn't risk letting the guy know with whom I was talking, in case he were her father.

"As you very well know, I am extremely poor in describing people's faces Ok? He looks exactly like Robert de Niro," she SMSed without short cuts. This she did when she was at her sarcastic best.

"Who is Robert de Niro?"

"This is why I always force you to watch English movies, but you never listen. You don't know Robert de Niro! He's my favorite. I told you this several times. I hate you," she typed back with proper punctuation and complete spellings. It indicated that she was getting irritated.

I was getting frustrated but couldn't help being sweet. The person next to me had to be Mr. Murlidhar, and in case he had missed the bus then his seat would have been allotted to some other guy.

"Does your dad dye his hair and does he have a moustache?"

"Why are you inquiring so much?"

"Just want to make sure that the person sitting next to me is your dad."

"He keeps moustache season wise and he dyes his hair often. He's ditto Robert de Niro."

"This time surely we will watch a movie of his. Will SMS you later, bye honey." Our chat was heading in a completely different direction. The information provided by her was of extremely little help. I decided to manage the things on my own. I couldn't have directly asked him either because if I did that and he turned out to be her father then he would have definitely asked me a hundred questions. He would be curious to know about the relationship I shared with Nisha. I wanted to impress him first and then reveal my identity. I also wanted to make him believe that he would never find a better groom for his daughter than me.

After some time, I found him taking a nap.

"Wow, Murli has taken 5 wickets in a test match. Wonderful!" I said loud enough to be heard by him. I pretended to focus on my cell phone. But the corner of my eye kept a watch on him. He remained undisturbed. If at all he were her father then he would surely react. Even he too was Murli after all.

"Murli, Murli," I said a bit louder this time as if I were cheering for Muttaih Murlitharan, the Sri Lankan cricketer. I pretended to focus on my cell phone screen but kept a watch on his movements through the corner of my eye. His eyes were open; he was giving a wild stare. His eyes were scary. I suddenly looked in an opposite direction. This is not the way to make an impression, my mind said. Moreover, Sri Lanka wasn't playing a match that day.

"Are you going to Bidar?" he asked suddenly.

"Yeah sir, this bus goes to Bidar. Are you going somewhere else?" my humor had not gone down well with him. But I considered it to be very funny. He just stared as if he were about to say something.

His phone started ringing. It was a gray colored latest model Nokia phone. He disconnected the call and kept it back in his pocket. Our bus was in Andhra Pradesh heading towards Hyderabad. Bidar was the last stop. Heavy roaming charges applied on Karnataka SIM cards in Andhra at that time. Call and SMS rates almost tripled, and people preferred to talk only if it were an emergency else the calls went unattended. Nisha had said that her father's mobile was stolen. If that were the case, then this person was not Mr. Murlidhar. But then he owned a chain of hotels in Bidar, and it was not a big deal for him to buy a new phone and get a duplicate SIM immediately. Again, his cell phone started ringing. He disconnected the call and kept it back in the pocket. Three hours had passed, and we were nearing the dhaba where the bus usually stopped. I had not yet ascertained the identity of the person next to me. I had the urge to ask him directly, and end the confusion. But then I didn't want to ruin things. I had to be cautious. The only possible explanation for his not picking the call was the roaming charges that applied. But then for a successful businessman like him, roaming charges shouldn't matter.

His cell phone started ringing again and before he could disconnect I intervened.

"Sir, I think you are pressing the wrong button. Just click on the green button, and you would be able to receive the call." His ringtone was like a cry of a thousand people trapped in a landslide. I developed migraine every time the phone rang. The people sitting in the nearby seats were also getting irritated by his frequent calls.

"Why don't you switch it off or put it into silent mode?" suggested a clever traveler.

"I am sorry," he said and disconnected it again.

"Give me ur dad's ph no," I sent her an SMS.

"9844 . . . . 22," luckily she was precise this time.

I prefixed a '0' and dialed the number.

His cell phone started ringing again. He once again repeated the same thing, disconnected it.

I repeated the act. Even he repeated the same. I felt like, Hritik Roshan of Kaho na pyar hai. All set to trap Anupam Kher in the climax. It was now proved beyond doubt that the person could either be Mr. Murlidhar or the thief himself. This realization sent chilling waves down my spine. I considered him a thief and planned my next course of action. It was evident that he wasn't picking any calls. Only a person who had stolen someone else's phone would have done that. It was 10:00 P.M. and the bus came to a halt.

"Dinner time," declared the conductor.

The passengers got down one by one. I decided to follow my neighbor, the thief. I decided to keep a strict vigil on him. He got down and started walking towards an open field on the other side of the road. I wondered what made him venture into the darkness. I observed him keenly from a distance. He cautiously crossed the road and reached the dark area. He then surveyed the area and headed towards a tree. Under the cover of the tree, he relieved himself. It took 2 minutes to empty his tank. Had he sensed that I was keeping a watch on him?

Was it a ploy to behave normally? Few others joined him in the vicinity, and they relieved together. In spite of the government constructing public toilets why did people prefer the open grounds? I failed to understand. I entered the dhaba and ordered a plate of paneer butter masala and 2 rotis.

As I waited for my order, I noticed him entering a telephone booth at a distance. The view was clear from where I was seated. He was talking with someone. He disconnected the call and dialed another number.

I received an SMS alert.

"Dad on hs way bk. He jst cld frm a tele booth," it was from Nisha.

Was the call made from the same booth? Was he her father?

My phone started ringing. It was an unknown number. I could see my suspect still ringing someone from the booth. He wasn't speaking though. I disconnected the call. I could see that he was dialing the number once again. My cell phone started ringing. I disconnected & switched off my cell phone. He tried once again in vain and came out without speaking. My hunger had vanished. I swiftly made an exit without waiting for the server to table my dish. I made sure that we didn't cross each other's path and vanished from his view.

There was no doubt after Nisha's SMS that he was indeed Mr. Murlidhar. I finalized my next course of action quickly. I saw him relaxing near the entrance of the bus.

"Sorry sir, sorry for the silly things I said."

He simply stared at me.

"Let me explain," I said. He listened intently.

"Your daughter Nisha is my friend. She had informed me about your journey in this bus. Later, I was informed that your luggage was stolen from the hotel room. We were actually worried if you would miss the bus. I was the one who gave you calls that you didn't receive. Since you were not receiving my calls, I believed you were the thief. My only motive was to establish your identity that's all. I just wanted to grill the thief and catch the offender. Hope you understand me," I said in one breath.

After a few seconds silence, he laughed monstrously & continuously as if I had cracked the joke of the day.

"His laugh is awesome and freaky," she had said while describing him.

I too joined him but failed to match his intensity.

"Oh poor boy," he said patting my back, "Young detective at work eh?"

I nodded. I made him laugh, and that made me feel proud. But I failed to understand what was so humorous about whatever I had told him.

"Since when do you know each other," he asked once inside the bus.

"We were classmates during our twelfth."

"I see, I see."

"Then?" I asked him as if I were waiting for his next query.

"What do you study now?"

"I just finished my final year engineering exams. I am also placed in a MNC, Infotech ltd," I said proudly.

"Congrats. You seem to be a bright student."

"Yes, I always stood first in class and did my engineering from a top college in Karnataka."

"Nisha always makes intelligent choices," he said. There was an instant wide grin on my face, which I tried to hide and behave normally.

"Friendship with her was one the best decisions of my life. The other best decision was to tell you everything tonight and have the privilege of interacting with you for the first time. I have this habit of making quick decisions, and they always prove to be right," I said with an air of pride.

"A decision cannot be right or wrong. The situations force us to make decisions," he said.

I remained silent.

"Making friendship with Nisha might have been really a good decision, but discussing it with me certainly wasn't," he said.

I turned pale. Was he angry that I was close to his beautiful daughter? We were so close that she was in continuous touch with me. There was no need for her to tell me that her father was also traveling in the same bus if she were just a friend.

"Sorry sir. I didn't get it," I said cautiously.

"Forget it. I have this habit of cracking complex jokes."

This relaxed me a bit.

"Uncle, I need to ask you something." I had cleverly made the journey from sir to uncle.

"Sure."

"Why weren't you picking the calls in the bus? It really created great confusion."

"My balance is low. I couldn't afford to lose the existing little balance while roaming. I am saving it for an emergency," he clarified.

I appreciated his wishful thinking.

"Can I use your cell phone for some time? I need to make an urgent call," he said. I immediately took my cell phone and gave it to him without a second thought, as if it were his. But the urge to impress him had made me commit a blunder. What if he reads the sweet messages exchanged between me and Nisha? We would be then caught red handed. Did he honestly want to make an emergency call or was it just a ploy to sneak into my private inbox. My heart pumped faster. I literally felt it.

"You seem to be sweating a lot. Have some water," he offered me his water bottle. I gulped it.

The melodious music of a Hindi song woke me up from a deep slumber. The bus driver had played the music to wake up the customers. I stretched both my arms and rubbed my eyes. The early morning sun looked red and calm. It was lush green and misty outside. I glanced at my left wrist, to check the time. The watch was missing. The seat next to me was vacant. To my horror my wallet was also missing. My heart beat tried to match the previous night's pace. It beat faster than before. I turned my face upwards for a breather. There was no luggage in the luggage rest. I ran to the bus conductor.

"Where is the person seated to my right?"

"He checked out two stops earlier."

"He stole all my belongings," I screamed, "Take the bus back to that place."

"We have come a long way. It's too late."

"What the hell! I will sue you for negligence," I threatened him at the top of my voice.

"You gave him your cell phone, right? Didn't you suspect him to be a thief then?" said a passenger seated at a distance to my right, defending the bus conductor.

"You saw me giving him the cell phone?"

"Yes."

"Then why the hell did you not see him stealing my belongings," I screamed.

"I was sleeping."

"Hello Mr. whoever you are, don't create a scene here. It's your mistake entirely," the conductor said. Few people sympathized with me and a few others discussed how foolish I was.

I reached home empty handed to the astonishment of my parents and shelved out the auto bill from my father's pocket. I looked like someone who had returned from a morning walk. There was not even a hand bag with me. I was wearing sports shoes.

"What happened?" asked my father.

"My decision making ability had gone for a toss last night."

"Nitin, my son, what happened?" asked my worried mother.

"A thief made me Bakra," I asserted again making slight changes to my earlier reply.

"Where is sahib's luggage?" said Janaki, my maid.

"Are you deaf?" I shot back and headed straight to my room.

My parents, maid, milkman, driver, gardener, my dog, & even its puppies sympathized with my situation.

I called up Nisha from the landline extension. It was 7:30 A.M.

"Nitin here," I said.

"Good morning. How was the journey?" she said excitedly.

"Quite memorable," I said without meaning it.

"We are expecting dad around 8:00 A.M. Since, he left 30 minutes later than you."

"30 minutes later? He called you around 10:00 P.M. or maybe 10:10 right?"

"He had called around 9:30 P.M."

"But I received your SMS at around 10:10."

"The SMSes are never delivered on time while roaming," she said, "Does the time at which he called really matter? Whether 10:10 or 9:30."

It did matter. The time had never mattered so much to me before. If only I had received her SMS earlier than he had entered the telephone booth, I would have unquestionably grilled the thief. It was a golden opportunity gone waste. I now cursed the cell phone service provider.

"Did your father tell you anything about the robbery?"

"Yeah, he said the investigation was going on. A hotel staff is suspected to be involved in it."

"Did he lose anything precious?"

"He carries a lot of credit and debit cards. He wants to ensure that they are deactivated at the earliest. So, he headed back in the evening itself for discussing the issue with the bank managers, in Bidar."

"And why didn't he board the bus I was in?"

"He didn't want to make you nervous," she giggled. "You are behaving too much. How would I know all that? I can only guess."

"How did he purchase a new ticket when he lost all his cash?"

"Hello Mr. Bond, will you please stop it?" she said irritably.

"I think I need some rest," saying that I disconnected the call abruptly and removed the extension wire. She would have tried calling on my cell phone which was with the thief. I lay on my bed recollecting the events that led to a disastrous journey. 'Congrats. You seem to be a bright student. A decision cannot be right or wrong. The situations force us to make decisions. Making friendship with Nisha might have been really a good decision, but discussing it with me certainly wasn't. Can I use your cell for some time? I need to make an urgent call.' I viewed these responses of his in the correct context this time. He had dropped enough hints. I failed to catch even one. He was far more intelligent than what I boosted of myself. Introducing me was one decision, which I would have to regret the rest of my life. "You seem to be sweating a lot. Have some water," he had said. My heart beat had increased after handing him the cell phone. There was no way; I would have gone into a deep slumber. Did the water work like a sleeping potion? Obviously! But there was something which troubled me more. What made him travel in the first place?

THE END

SWEET REVENGE

I realized that the situation had gone out of control. He held her hand forcibly. She pleaded and tried hard to free herself from his clutches. He tried to embrace her. She pushed him but in vain. The blood in my veins was surging. I was helpless but not a coward. I couldn't be just a spectator anymore. He was 6 feet, heavily built middle aged man. I was thin, short at that time, aged 10. I looked around for a weapon. But our tiny shed had some kitchen utensils, clothes placed in a trunk, and a leaky bucket apart from my prized marbles which I had won from Pakkya & other friends in the locality. Father was in the small partitioned section of our tiny shed, unaware of the happenings around him. He had been fully drunk that night, as always. Until the next morning, there was no chance of him regaining consciousness. Beside him lay a dozen beer bottles. All empty.

He was trying to smooch her. "Ranganna be careful," I warned in rage, standing at a feet's distance.

He looked at me in amusement. "You tiny little filthy son of a bitch, what audacity you worm!" he said and slapped me with his mighty hand.

I fell on the floor.

"Don't hit him, he's just a child. I beg your pardon," she pleaded in desperation.

"Don't you dare speak to me in that tone," he thundered at me. "You will have to pay with that only piece of cloth on your body. I will make you a laughing stock if you don't leave the place now." I was wearing only shorts, which mother had gifted on my birthday. It was torn at parts which were meant to be covered and protected. Our poverty was such that she had stitched those torn portions using a piece of her sari.

"Don't hurt my mother," I warned him again, controlling my tears. The slap had turned my cheek red. The feeling of helplessness was making me more and more desperate with every passing moment.

"Putta, son, you don't get into this," mother pleaded.

"You scoundrel, won't you obey your mother?" he said with a wicked smile.

I entered the partitioned portion of the shed.

"What an obedient son and an equally understanding mother," he taunted and burst into evil laughter.

Father was a drunkard since the day I've known him. Nobody in the slum liked him because of his habits and arrogant attitude. He would fight with anyone who came forward to preach sanity. He would come home drunk regularly in the night, abuse mother and beat her up mercilessly. Whatever little money she earned as a maid would be snatched by him on a regular basis. We lived in one of the biggest slums in Bangalore and he worked as a server in a liquor shop, in the busy market area. Ranganna owned the shop. Father borrowed money from him apart from his regular salary, on one or the other pretext, but could never return. The debt only grew. Ranganna visited the house frequently threatening and abusing us. He had developed a liking for mother. His visit would enrage me, and I developed a strong dislike for him. Mother sobbed, each time he harassed us and left, cursing her fate.

"I will definitely take the revenge mother," I would say and pacify her. It was enough to comfort her, and she would hug me.

"You are my only ray of hope, but he is a dangerous man. Stay away from him," she would caution. Mother was mild and innocent. She would never fight with the father, but he made it a point to hurt her for no reason. On several occasions, I was beaten up by the father in my effort to save her. This pained her more. I secretly vowed to destroy Ranganna and his liquor shop which was the sole reason for the constant pain and suffering of mother.

This was the best chance to take revenge. Mother's pleas and his wicked smile drove me crazy. I finally gathered courage and the weapon.

I patted on his back. He turned around. Almost instantly a big beer bottle crashed on his head like a coconut and shattered into pieces. The impact was such that blood oozed out of his head in no time. He fell on the ground. The inverted bucket made sure that I matched his height. The execution was successful. Mother hugged me. I had never seen her so happy in a very long time. After the joy had sufficed, we looked at the still Ranganna. There was an expression of horror on her face.

"Hope he's not dead," she whispered and hurried to check. "Thank god, he's still alive." We poured a bucket full of water on him. His body moved. He was shaky yet managed to get up on his own. I stood next to him on the base of the bucket with a new beer bottle all set to strike. I was more confident this time. Mother was by my side. He stared at us for a long time. Without speaking a word, he made an unceremonious exit in the dark. Mother spent the entire night worrying about the consequences of my action. She was of the firm belief that he would strike back in vengeance. She worried for my safety. She cleaned up the blood stains and the shattered pieces of glass.

Father came back to senses the next morning. He had no clue about last night's incident. I anticipated him to create a big ruckus on his return from work that night. Mother wore a worried look the entire day and skipped work fearing for my safety. She also made plans to send me to my aunt's house in a far away slum in the city.

"I wouldn't leave you and go," I declared. She needed me more than before.

Father returned as usual, drunk. He bore injury marks on the body. He didn't utter a word upon arrival and maintained an uncanny silence. Mother was feeling the pressure. The sweat on her forehead, the unusual urgency in the way she did things, and the tense expression on her face indicated how uncomfortable she was on his arrival.

"You seem to be hurt very badly, what happened?" asked my concerned mother. He held her by her thick long hairs and pulled her to his side, which surely pained as she yelled.

"What did you and your filthy son do to Ranganna last night?"

"He was misbehaving with me. I pleaded him several times but . . ." she said.

"What did you do to ignite his lust?"

"What are you talking?"

I was patiently listening to their conversation. My patience had reached the threshold. The everyday drama had to end one day. His fist suddenly landed on her face and dealt a severe blow. Blood trickled from her nose. It was nasty.

I ran towards him in anger. The next moment, a beer bottle, found its target. It shattered into two pieces upon landing forcefully on his head. The impact was such that he fell on the ground instantly. Luckily, there was no blood. All his blood seems to have transformed into alcohol, I presumed. Mother cried in desperation.

"What have you done?" she asked in panic. The next moment she went outside, looking for help. I had never seen him so calm. It was the second time I had hit someone in two days. Was I turning into a devil? Not even a single drop of tear appeared in my eyes. What did he do to gain sympathy? Apart from abusing and giving us a life of utter poverty, he had achieved nothing. Our life was a living hell. Only he was responsible for all the mess. I checked his breath and shook him violently. Fortunately, he opened eyes after half an hour of continuous effort.

"Are you ok?" I asked.

He stared at me in disbelief & anger. The eyes were red. His head had swollen at the spot where I hit him.

Mother then arrived with a few neighboring aunties, four to be precise.

"Thank god he is alive," said one of them.

"Alcohol has turned this man into an animal!" shouted the other.

My mother trickled some water on his face and helped him stand. He was finding difficulty in balancing. He pushed her aside once he stood up looking at me in anger.

"Don't harm him, he is only a child," mother pleaded.

He remained silent for some time as if contemplating something. The ladies were continuously blabbering. His expression had now changed. Probably, he understood that he was in minority. The angry females were difficult to contain for him.

"Ranganna has vengeance in mind. He has summoned Putta to his home tonight," he said.

"Let's send him off to a safer place till Ranganna's anger subsides," said an old lady. I had resolved not to leave my mother alone. I believed it was a ploy by the father to send me away so that he could punish her for my bravery.

"I am not scared to meet him again," I said.

"I am not going to send my son to the monster's home," said mother.

"That's the only way, we can calm him down. He's furious over last night's incident," said father.

"Okay, then all of us will accompany Putta to Ranganna's place," said an elderly lady.

"It has to be only Putta," said father.

"I am not going to leave my son alone. I repeat," said mother.

"If we fail to do so, then we may have to leave the slum, and the city too," said father.

"Let's do it."

"Don't behave like a child. Leaving a city is no easy task. Where will we go?"

After much deliberation, the elders decided to send me along with father to Ranganna's place. If we failed to return in a few hours time, then they would report the matter to the cops. Mother believed that Ranganna surely would break one or more beer bottles on my head.

"He would take revenge for every drop of his spilled blood," she said.

"Don't worry, he's going along with his father," said one aunty.

It was dark, starless night. I sensed an unusual calmness in the surroundings. How would he take revenge? How painful it would be to receive a powerful hit on the head using a beer bottle? Will I be alive after that? Several such questions revolved in my mind. The huge gates of Ranganna's building were guarded by a giant rifled man. I had heard that Ranganna stayed in the big house with only his wife. The other portion of the house was rented.

"Sir is waiting for you. Head this way!" the guard said arrogantly pointing at the entrance of the house.

A knock on the door and his wife opened it. She greeted us with a smile. She was the first to have smiled looking at me, in several days, apart from my mother. I smiled too. She was much younger in age and wore a parrot green gown. My colorless life attracted me towards colors. Pakkya always said that green was the color for prosperity. Father nudged me to behave myself. He looked normal & was in his senses after getting hit by me, even though a part of his head had swollen significantly.

"So the filthy worm has finally arrived!" said Ranganna arrogantly. His head was covered in bandage. I felt proud of my brute force. He made us sit on the floor in a corner of the room. The large entrance housed a TV mounted upon the wall. A cushioned sofa and a glassy dining table lay at the other end. A number of alcohol bottles of different shapes and sizes occupied the table in front of him. He took one lazy sip every five minutes. We waited, for his drinks, to get over. His wife served him one plate full of roasted peanuts and finger chips. She then headed towards the kitchen. My mouth watered, but I controlled the urge. I had never been inside such a palatial place before. I envied Ranganna at that moment. We kept looking at him, but he behaved as if we didn't exist. He was watching some English movie. One hour passed by without any communication between us.

"Little bastard wants to know the reason why he's here?" he spoke finally.

"Please forgive him Anna. He is still a naive kid," father pleaded.

"Forgive him so easily? I cannot even open my mouth fully and grind these delicious chips because of his nasty strike. The skull aches."

Father elbowed me to beg for forgiveness. I brushed his gesture aside and maintained silence.

"Speak up you cockroach!" Ranganna screamed.

I remained silent.

"Creatures as you ought to be taught an apt lesson," he said and called out his wife. She appeared to smile.

"Get the special cocktail that you've prepared for this son of a bitch."

She looked at me sympathetically and asked him, "You think this little boy would be able to digest it?"

"Let him know how an alcohol tastes. I've already had my retribution on his father. Poor father suffered because of his stupid son. It's his turn now. Filthy little worm would never again break the bottle on others head when he realizes the preciousness of what it holds. Let him dare to break the bottle then. The bottle is precious because something inside is precious. It is not a weapon . . . ." She returned to the kitchen.

In a drunk state Ranganna kept on uttering so many senseless things. Had he planned to turn me into a drunkard too? So that I would visit his wine shop regularly like my father did and he could target my mother again. Ranganna was not in his senses. He tried keeping the wine glass on the table and missed. The glass fell and the alcohol spilled near his foot. My father got up to clean the mess, but the enraged Ranganna abused him and ordered not to leave the place without permission.

His wife appeared with a bottle full of dark brownish liquid and an empty glass. She headed straight towards me and suggested pouring the liquid in the glass.

"Let me drink this poison on my son's behalf, show sympathies Anna," father said. I knew his mouth watered at the sight of the drink. He wouldn't have ever missed such a golden opportunity to get drunk for free.

"It's strictly for your son," she warned and gave him a stern look.

Father headed towards Ranganna and held his feet, begging for a chance to take my punishment upon him. Ranganna kicked him in the chest, and he fell exactly where the alcohol had spilled sometime ago. I saw him licking the floor. His chances of improving looked dismal.

"Gulp it," Ranganna told me in half wakefulness.

I hesitated, but there was no option. The drink was a little sweetish. The soda strangely tasted better. I started with smaller sips, and once the hesitation withered away, I consumed larger gulps. The glass was empty in few seconds. My thirst had increased. I projected the glass towards her, gesturing her to pour more. Her eyes widened. She served me another drink with a smile. I guess it surprised her.

"Anna, please let me sip only a quarter," father begged. He was returning to his true self.

"It's only meant for the little bastard, and I am glad that he likes it," Ranganna said with a wicked smile.

This was the first time in my life I was tasting alcohol, and I really enjoyed it. After two, servings, I anticipated to experience the immediate consequences of it. I had seen many drunkards, especially father, finding it difficult to hold the ground and puke all over the place. Few others like Ranganna spoke nonsense when drunk. Another thing I observed was that a drunkard always has a sound sleep irrespective of what happened around. He is like a dead man. And above all a drunkard would always utter the filthiest of abuses.

'If only I get out of control, then I would repay Ranganna with a barrage of abuses which would target his mother too. I would have to spare his wife as she had been a sweet hostess. Ranganna cannot even accuse me of being abusive. Later, I would claim to have been under the influence of alcohol,' I thought.

It was my fourth straight serving. She looked at me in amazement every time I gestured her to pour some more. I burped louder than before, each time I completed drinking a glass. Ranganna was totally out of his senses. In spite of drinking so much, I was fully aware of the surroundings and in control of myself. The alcohol didn't seem to affect me in any way. I walked certain distance to check if I could hold the ground. My eye sight was perfect. I deserved something stronger than that.

"You filthy son of a bitch," I suddenly screamed at Ranganna. I pretended to lose balance as I walked towards him. My tone was that of a drunken man. I had learnt it by observing father. He looked at me in shock. After, consuming four glasses of cocktail for the first time, anybody could have lost his senses. For others in the room, I was a drunken kid. I had to act perfectly, or else there were chances of his smart wife identifying the truth. Nobody apart from father & Ranganna had abused me using the choicest of abuses. It was payback time.

"What the hell?" Ranganna said. His eyes were finding it difficult to keep themselves open. He stood in anger while indicating with his raised arm that he was about to hit me. His legs were shaky. The next moment he fell on the floor. He uttered a few things which can at best be termed meaningless. He kept muttering to himself. I regretted that I hadn't got enough chances to take my revenge.

She hurried towards him and then there was a knock on the door. The subsequent knocks were louder and rapid than before. She gestured me to open the door as she provided physical support for her slipped husband.

Two police constables, a cameraman, a reporter along with my mother and the four neighboring aunties entered the room as I opened the door. The camera was on, the moment they entered. The reporter began his running commentary. "Our channel is the first to report this barbarous incident," he said. I felt like a celebrity. I had once seen how the same channel had covered the entire episode of Pakkya's dramatic fall into a deep pit and his successful rescue.

"Putta, are you alright?" My mother asked. She hugged me the next moment & kissed on my face hurriedly. She was making sure that I wasn't tortured physically. I hugged her tightly.

"Arrest this fellow. He is holding our Putta hostage for the past three hours," said an elderly lady pointing at Ranganna. Father begged the police to leave Ranganna alone. My mother stared at him in anger for the first time.

"Stop behaving like a dog and favor your son," she thundered. I just couldn't believe what I had heard. It boosted my morale.

"He made me drink several glasses of cocktail and abused me," I said pointing at Ranganna.

The constables slapped and arrested him.

"You fed alcohol to this innocent kid? Have you forgotten all the traits of humanity?" said the pot-bellied constable. I wondered what resulted in such a perfect shaped belly. They took him away, within minutes, in a waiting police jeep. The aunties celebrated the demon's arrest. They accused father of behaving like Ranganna's agent while delivering him sermon on how to support the family. The reporter geared up to interview me. The only strange thing was that Ranganna's wife had not resisted his arrest. She didn't utter anything in her husband's defense and was seated on the dining chair. She had maintained silence throughout the ensuing dramatic developments.

I headed towards her.

"Ranganna is evil, but you are a nice lady," I said.

She smiled.

"Are you not angry that he was arrested because of me?"

"I could sense the direction in which he was headed, given the kind of things he does. To be frank he deserved it," she said.

"I feel sorry for you."

She ignored my comment with a smile and said, "You are a bright boy. And you act well!"

"Sorry?"

"It wasn't alcohol. I served you a cola drink. I wouldn't create another drunkard with my own hands."

I was speechless. Just then the reporter positioned the camera in front of me and my interview commenced.

"I am feeling dizzy. Ranganna forcibly served a heavy drink with his own hands . . . ." I began.

THE END